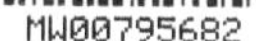
MW00795682

BOOK 3
TOBY ANDREWS
AND THE
JUNIOR
DEPUTIES
THE
EAST SIDE
BULLIES

JERRY B. JENKINS

Author of The Dallas O'Neill Mystery Series

MOODY PRESS
CHICAGO

ISBN: 0-8024-1627-6

1 3 5 7 9 10 8 6 4 2

Printed in the United States of America

To those who rescue
others from bullies

Contents

The Price of Fame

The Kalamazoo County Junior Deputies usually meet only on Sunday afternoons. I was elected captain, probably because the deputies were my dad's idea and we meet at my house. The four other guys in the group (plus my little sister, Kate) all go to the same church we do. And Old Tom (my nickname for Thomas Christian), the lieutenant, almost always has Sunday dinner at our house.

I call him Old Tom because he looks so much older than he is. Thomas and I are both twelve, but he looks as if he could already have a driver's license. He's tall and dark-haired, and his face has that chiseled look of somebody who is already mature. He's strong too.

On Sunday mornings—and sometimes the day before—my parents sign him out of the kids' Home where he lives, and he spends the day with us. He goes to church with us, eats at our place, and we play together until he has to be back at the Lake Farm Home. He's my best friend.

I've known the other three guys longer, because we all

grew up in the same church, but Thomas and I have somehow just become closer. We're in the same grade at the same school, but not in the same class. Still, we see each other every day.

I have nicknames for the other guys too. I call Jonathan Bynum Red Jon because of his red hair. He could have all kinds of nicknames because he's so funny and goofy. His skin is chalky white, and he can't stay out in the sun very long. He has a huge smile and a silly laugh. Since he looks like that, I guess it makes sense that he doesn't usually take anything too seriously.

Daniel Jackson, our black friend, I call Big Dan for obvious reasons. He's bigger and rounder than Old Tom, but nobody makes the mistake of thinking he's older. He's still got a young-looking face, all wide-eyed and with teeth that look too big for his mouth. That's true of all of us except Old Tom. My mom says we haven't grown into our teeth yet.

Then there's Joel McBride. I call him Little Joel. He's only ten, but he's been in our group for as long as I can remember. In fact, I can't remember when I met Little Joel. I've been running around in the parking lot after church for so long that I have no idea when it started. All I know is, Joel has always been the fastest kid out there, his blond hair flying as he catches the older kids and is impossible to catch himself.

I don't have a nickname for Kate. At least not one I would put in a book. I'm not supposed to call her names, even though she drives me crazy sometimes. It's not as bad as it used to be. We treat each other better now that our big brother, Jason, is gone. He died of cancer when he was sixteen, and I think it made both Kate and me realize how short life can be and what we really mean to each other.

Kate's two years younger than Joel, so she hasn't been involved in any of our cases. But still, she's a Kalamazoo County Junior Deputy with a badge to prove it. Kate usually gets tired of sitting in our meetings and finally runs off to play, and that's sort of the way we want it. It's one thing to have the captain's little sister as part of the group, but it would be awful if she had to be in on everything.

The club got started because I think my dad got tired of us asking him too many questions about police work. He's a deputy with the Kalamazoo County Sheriff's office.

It wasn't long after we started our little club that we helped solve a case and got our names in the *Kalamazoo Gazette.* Some guy had hidden stolen stuff in the tunnels under our new house, and we helped lure him back to get it while Dad and his men waited to arrest him.

It was pretty cool to be known as heroes, and we got a few more cases out of it after the story appeared in the *Gazette.* Mostly we had friends and classmates ask us to help them with little problems, like who stole their sports equipment or tore their coat or hit them with a snowball.

That last was a funny one, because for a while I was so impressed with myself as a junior deputy that I almost made a fool of myself. Well, not almost. I did make a fool of myself.

A girl I kind of liked (though I never admitted it), Pam Zibell, was hit on the cheek by a snowball. Everybody knew Randy Hendricks had done it, and there had even been a couple of eyewitnesses. But at first Randy denied it, and it seemed clear that Pam just wanted to drop it.

But by now I had been in the paper and was known as the head of the Junior Deputies, so I went to Pam, all self-important-like. I said, "I can investigate this, or I can leave it alone. It's up to you."

She looked at me like I was from another planet. "Investigate it?" she repeated. "How would you do that?"

"I'd re-create the scene. You show me where you were standing, and I'll try to determine the trajectory of the snowball and—"

"You'll what the what?" she said. "Toby Andrews, you've been reading too many stories."

"I'll determine the trajectory," I said. "You know—the angle. I'll ask people who saw it which direction the snowball came from, and you can tell me which way you were facing. Then I can find out who was standing where and narrow it down to a few suspects."

Pam was not impressed. She just sat there shaking her head and rubbing her red cheek.

"He could have put your eye out," I said.

"Who could have?"

"Whoever did this."

"You're sure it was a guy?" she said. "How do you know it wasn't a girl?"

"Well, I don't yet, but—"

"And we always hear about people getting their eyes put out from a snowball," she said, "but have you ever known anyone who was actually hurt by a snowball?"

"No, but—"

"Then just leave this alone," Pam said. "I can tell from how Randy looks that he did it and that he feels bad about it."

"Yeah, but I could prove it. With string and a tape measure I could—"

Pam looked over my shoulder. I turned to see Randy towering over me.

"The people who tell you which way the snowball came from will also tell you who threw it," he said, "won't they?"

I shrugged as Pam laughed. "I guess they would."

"Then we don't need Sherlock Holmes, do we?" he said, and lots of kids laughed.

I knew I was turning red.

"*I* threw the snowball," Randy said. "Everybody knows it, including Pam."

"I wasn't sure," she said, embarrassed, looking at Randy as if she were impressed.

"How many times have I hit you in the side or in the back this week?" he asked.

"Lots," she admitted.

"And how many times have you tried to get me back?" he asked.

"Lots," she said, "but you move too quick."

"Well, I'm sorry I hit you in the face. I didn't mean to."

"I know."

"So I'll quit throwing at you."

"Thanks."

It was clear I was not needed.

"Why don't you take credit for this, Andrews?" Randy said. "You can get your name and your picture in the paper again. You'll be a big hero one more time. You investigated and then got the criminal and victim together for a chat."

I might have been an OK junior deputy, but I wasn't good at comebacks to insults. I slunk back to my desk, hearing giggles.

Later that week was Valentine's Day, and though the whole class was supposed to send cards to each other, Randy and Pam sent cards only to each other. Maybe I should have plunked her in the face with a snowball instead of trying to rescue her.

That spring Thomas and I helped the police catch a man who worked at Lake Farm and who had two wives at the same time. That story made the Junior Deputies even more famous, but it led to a real problem for us too. This time it was more than just classmates teasing us.

Although it was only Thomas and I who were involved in the case of the man with two wives, after two news stories about us, the *Gazette* sent a writer to do a feature on the Junior Deputies. It listed all our names and ages, even Kate's.

The biggest deal was made, of course, about the fact that the son of a sheriff's deputy was in charge of the group. The article told all about our Victorian house and the tunnels we had discovered in the basement when we moved in.

Even though we live in Kalamazoo, Michigan, our house had been used decades before by some mobsters connected with a Chicago gang. Back in the years when it was illegal to buy and sell liquor, they ran booze out of the house by storing it in the basement and carrying it through the tunnels to their cars in the garage.

The tunnels ran from an old coal bin, which was where we now held our Junior Deputy club meetings. The newspaper carried a picture of the six of us, and just to be funny, I guess, they asked us to all wear our badges. We never wore badges, of course, but my dad had given us souvenir ones he had traded for with other police departments. We carried them but were never supposed to flash them or use them. That part of it was just for fun.

But there we stood in the newspaper picture, four twelve-year-old boys, one ten-year-old boy, and an eight-year-old girl, hands on our hips, badges shining on our chests. We'd been mentioned before in the paper, but this really made us famous. The article quoted me, saying that we were in business and looking for cases.

I should have realized that something was wrong when the attention from all that came mostly from adults. Relatives, friends of my parents, people at church, and teachers all said nice things to me. And the other deputies had the same thing happen. But other kids just didn't seem that impressed.

I tried to figure that out. I wondered how I would feel if someone else in my class was featured in a big story in the paper. I liked to think I would be thrilled for them. Once a girl in my class was pictured with her cousin. They had found some four-leaf clovers. I thought that was pretty neat, but as I thought about it, it was nothing to be jealous of. I had never even looked for four-leaf clovers.

I was jealous of her for having her picture in the paper, though. And I had to admit I was jealous of a kid in the other sixth-grade class, Thomas's class, when he had his picture taken at the state capitol, shaking hands with a senator.

So that had to be it. The reason we got praised from adults was because they thought we were industrious. I heard that word so many times, I had to look it up. It meant we were "hardworking and ambitious." The reason we got either no reaction or a bad reaction from kids was that they were jealous. They sure didn't want us to think we were something special. They knew we were just like them except that we had done something that older people thought was cute. That was sort of the worst thing a kid could do and still be cool.

The problem with fame is that the more you get, the more you want. I had wanted to be a hero, and in a way we all had been. Three articles in the paper should have been all we ever needed. But my dreams were bigger. I imagined catching a crook by myself, saving someone's life, being on the TV news.

I didn't tell my family or the other kids, of course, but what would have been better than to have a parade in my honor, maybe be carried through the streets on people's shoulders? A guy can dream. I knew there was no humility in my dreams. That's why they were dreams. And I knew they were silly. I already had all the fame I was ever likely to get, and it was not at all what I had expected. I thought it would make me more popular and well-known. Well, I had become well-known. I wouldn't say it had made me popular. In fact, all that attention got me, and my friends, and my sister, into big trouble.

That was why we had to call an emergency meeting one Saturday afternoon last spring. Thomas was going to be at my house Saturday and Sunday as usual, so we called to see if Big Dan, Red Jon, and Little Joel could come over for a special get-together.

“Does this mean we’re not meetin’ Sunday afternoon?” Daniel wanted to know.

“We may have to meet then too,” I told him. “After what happened, we may have to meet a lot for a while.”

“After what happened,” Daniel repeated, “we ought to do more than just meet and talk.”

I couldn’t have agreed more.

The Threat

It had taken several weeks to clean out the old coal bin to the point where my mom agreed to let us meet there. In fact, after we went through every rag and old towel in the house trying to get years of coal dust off the walls and floor, my dad finally let us use the sprayer on the hose to really get the place clean.

Then we made a mess of painting the room, ceiling and floor and all, pure white. Man, did it look different! It still had only one light bulb hanging from the middle of the ceiling, but what a change because of the white paint! It must have been ten times brighter in there, and the room looked bigger too.

Mom let us have an old coffee table, a beat-up old couch, and a bunch of cheap folding chairs. That was all we needed. Mostly we just sat around and talked or played games in there. On Sundays we had our official weekly meeting. But that Saturday we were not in a playing or "just talking" mood.

My dad and I drove over to get Thomas that Saturday morning and sign him out. Thomas was a hero at Lake Farm. The man he and I had got fired from there had two families in two towns and had a criminal record of stealing money from his wives. None of the kids at Lake Farm liked him anyway, so they were glad to see him leave.

Thomas had already been a favorite at Lake Farm because he was a tough kid. And yet he was never mean. He would fight to defend himself or somebody else, but he never just fought to fight. He was a Christian and went to church with us every Sunday. And even though he was about in the middle of the age range at Lake Farm, he had a reputation as good as any of the older guys.

He wasn't much one for smiling. He was a pretty serious kid and had had a lot of trouble in his life. But usually, when he saw me or one of my parents, he might smile or look a little embarrassed when he said hi. But not that day. Though he considered us family and was always glad to get away from the Home, he knew our Saturday afternoon meeting was not about fun.

I had been looking forward to having the morning with Thomas alone, just to talk strategy, but I couldn't get him to talk. He just wanted to think or talk about something else. The other guys weren't coming until after lunch; still, Thomas wouldn't help me plan what we might do.

The reason for the meeting had come Friday night when I got a call from Joel McBride, the one I call Little Joel. He and Big Dan and Red Jon all go to the same school, Eastwood Elementary. At school Joel doesn't hang around Daniel and Jonathan because he's so much younger. At church and in the Junior Deputies we don't make a big deal about ages, so there's no problem. After what had happened Friday afternoon, though, Joel sure wished he'd been with Dan and Jon.

He had been heading for the bike rack after school when

he noticed three junior high kids on their bikes at the end of an alley across the street.

"That was strange," he told me on the phone. "We always get out twenty minutes earlier than the junior high, because they're three blocks away and we can get out of their way. We haven't had any trouble with Estes Junior High ever since they changed the times for the end of school."

"And?" I said.

"And when I got to my bike, there were two locks on it."

"Two? One was yours, right?"

"Sure. But I had never even seen the other one. It was one of those big, black, front-tire collar jobs, and it was wrapped through the spokes and the struts and around two bars in the rack. 'Course, I wouldn't have been able to get it off anyway."

"What did you do?"

"What could I do? I thought it was a joke. I said, 'Who's the wise guy?' I tried to act like it was funny and that it was all right, as long as somebody would come and take it off. Only thing was, it didn't look like any lock I had seen before. I've seen 'em in stores, but none of my friends had one like it. The only thing that even looked like it was a red one that Dave Snyder has. I asked him if it was his, and he said no. He unlocked his bike and took off. After about five minutes I was the only one standing there. Everyone else had gotten their bikes and left. I didn't know how long it would take to saw through that lock, even if I found someone to do it.

"I didn't know what else to do, so I went back into the school and went to the office. Nobody there knew anything about it, and they said I should talk to Mr. Gaylor—the custodian. He came out with me to look at it and said he didn't think a normal hacksaw would cut through it. He said anyway he thought it was a practical joke and that no one would want such a nice lock cut through.

"I said, 'What am I supposed to do?'

"He said, 'Call your parents.'

"Well, you know I wasn't going to do that. I followed him back into the building, which must have made the junior highers think we were going to get some sort of a tool to cut it with."

"How do you know that?"

"Because when I came back out alone, the lock was loose."

"It was?"

"Yup. It was still on there, but it was open. I couldn't figure it out. I hadn't even thought about those older kids on bikes having anything to do with it, but there was no one else around. They were still watching—and laughing. That scared me. I didn't know what they were up to, so I just pulled the lock off and set it on the ground. But as I backed my bike out of the rack, those guys came across the street.

"One of them yelled, 'What are you doin' with my lock?'

"I didn't even answer. I just pushed my bike back into the rack and slipped my lock back onto it. Then I took off running."

"Running! Did you think you could outrun *bikes?"*

"I knew I could. I didn't have time to get on my bike and build up any speed, but I could go where bikes couldn't, so I did. I jumped over bushes and went between tight places where they couldn't follow. I made it back into the school, but I didn't want to squeal on them, so I just waited till they left. I saw them out the window picking up their lock. As they rode off, one of them kicked the spokes on the back tire of my bike. Broke two and dented two."

"Why?"

"I didn't have any idea, but I sure didn't want to go back out there until they were gone. I waited about ten more minutes. Mr. Gaylor said, 'You still here? You want me to call someone?' I told him, 'No, I'm just leaving. You were right. It was just someone having fun with me.'

"When I went back out, I was scared to death. It felt like I was being watched. I kept looking around, but I didn't see anybody—until I was on my bike, and then I couldn't go fast enough to get away."

"Who'd you see?"

"Those same guys. They were down the street a ways but behind some trees. I saw them peeking out. I acted like I didn't see them and sort of casually started riding away. I glanced back to see where they were, and they hadn't moved yet. Once I got up a little speed, I really raced. I knew I could outrun them on foot, but there was no way I could stay ahead of them for a mile until I got home. I just made sure I stayed on main streets and didn't take any shortcuts."

"Why? Couldn't you have outrun them if they didn't know where they were going?"

"Maybe, but if they caught me in an alley or on a side street, I wouldn't have any witnesses."

"Where'd they catch you?"

"Just past the dairy."

"There must have been lots of traffic."

"There was. That's probably why they didn't beat me up."

"What'd they do?"

"Pushed me around a little, acted like they were just playing. Nobody would have thought anything about it."

"What did they say?"

"They kept calling me 'junior deputy.'"

"You're kidding!"

"Nope. They said, 'What were you doing with our lock, Junior Deputy?' I said I didn't do anything with it. They asked if I thought I was tough because I was a junior deputy. I said no, I just wanted to go home. They asked me if I was going to cry, and Toby, I would have if they hadn't asked me that. I said, 'No, I'm not afraid of you.' I have no idea why I said that because I was never more afraid in my whole life.

"One of 'em said, 'Well, maybe you *ought* to be afraid of us,' and he picked up the front tire of my bike and tipped me back like I was doing a wheelie. I was hanging on for dear life, trying not to fall off. He says, 'You want me to put you down?' I said, 'Yes!' And he let go. The front tire banged down, and I lost my balance and tipped over. I scraped my hand and bumped my head a little. But as I was getting up, one of them scooted forward and ran his tire up my leg. I've got a tire burn on my calf."

"And nobody saw this?"

"Uh-uh. It just looked like a bunch of kids horsing around."

"Was that it?"

"No. They said that next time I saw their lock on my bike, I should assume it's their bike. I said, 'But it's not your bike, and next time your lock is on it, I'm going to cut it off.'"

"You said that, Joel? Man!"

"I didn't feel as brave as I sounded. That's when the biggest one punched me in the arm. I've got a big bruise. Toby, you know my dad would kill me or them or both. I can't tell him. But we've got to do something. That guy said they were gonna start picking us off one by one."

"Picking who off?"

"The Junior Deputies. He called me that a lot of times and then said something about 'you heroes thinkin' you're such big shots.' He said, 'You won't think that when we get through with you.'"

"I wonder what their problem is with us," I said.

"No idea," Joel said, "but we'd better let the other guys know."

And that was why we were meeting the day before our usual time. I told Joel to come right at one o'clock. I knew he would probably be the last one there.

Daniel had to get a ride because he lived the farthest away, and he showed up when Thomas and I had just finished lunch. He had an interesting idea.

"Know what?" he said. "From what you told me, I don't think your sister needs to know about this. Those bullies from the East Side are not going to bother her, and she might tell your parents. Our reputation will be mud if we tell on somebody just because they threaten us."

Thomas and I nodded.

"How do we keep her out of it?" Thomas asked.

"Just talk about a bunch of boring stuff until she gets tired of sitting there," Big Dan suggested. "When she goes off to play, we can get down to business. And I hope that business includes standing up to those guys."

"Who knows how many of them there are?" I said. "Or how old or how big?"

"They can't be that much bigger than Thomas and me," Daniel said, which was hard to argue with.

"But do we really want to get into a fight?" I asked.

"'Course not," Thomas said. "But we may not have a choice. I agree with not telling on them, though. We get them in trouble, and they may still come after us. We have to fight our own battles."

The conversation changed when redheaded Jonathan Bynum showed up. "This is too cool!" he said. "We have real enemies? Can we ambush 'em? Practical joke 'em? Scare 'em? What?"

I started thinking about how strange it was that we were all church kids. We were Christians. Our whole club started because we were friends from church. And here we were, even before the victim got there, talking about how we were going to get back at the guys who did this to Joel and who might do the same to the rest of us.

I didn't want to sound like Joe Sunday School, but I did wonder what this had to do with being like Jesus, turning the other cheek, and all that.

Jonathan reminded me that even Jesus got mad and kicked the money changers out of the temple. "And I've read other places," Jon added, "where pastors are told to act like gatekeepers of the sheep and to fight off any attackers."

"But we're not pastors," I said. "And we don't want adults fighting for us. What are we supposed to do?"

The Emergency Meeting

I decided not to mention my thoughts about how revenge fit with the kind of kids we were supposed to be, at least not until Joel got there and everybody heard the whole story at once. Just as I figured, he arrived at about 1:15. He had a bruise on the side of his head, and he showed us the tire burn on his leg.

"How'd you get that?" Kate asked.

Joel had always liked Kate, though he never admitted it. He started to tell her how he got it, but then I guess he realized that I must have not told her on purpose. "It happened when I fell off my bike," he said.

That satisfied her.

I pulled him off to the side as we headed downstairs to the old coal bin. "We're going to just talk business until Kate wanders off. She doesn't need to know what happened to you."

He nodded. "She'd probably tell anyway. Then I'd really be in for it."

There were things that should never get back to Joel's parents. His mother was a Christian and always took him to church. But his dad was a mean guy who came to church only at Christmas and Easter. When he dressed up in a suit he looked like the most uncomfortable person in the world. We heard he fought in Vietnam and saw so many horrible things that he turned his back on God and didn't want anything to do with church.

The problem is, he and his wife had grown up in the same church and were engaged before he left for the war. When he got back, they were married, but soon she didn't recognize him as the same boy. It was all she could do to get him to come to church even for holidays. He was often prayed for and visited by the pastors, but he never seemed to change.

Joel never talked much about his father, but we knew he was often drunk. Joel said he never felt he was actually abused, but when he got in trouble his dad yelled and screamed and locked him in his room. A couple of times he felt his dad's spankings went too far, but Joel was afraid to report it—and so was his mother, who had been hit a few times herself.

We were all afraid of Joel's dad, but he sure seemed like a nice guy when he was sober. Joel said he was always apologizing when he wasn't drunk, and Joel and his mother wanted so bad to forgive him and see him change that they just kept giving him second chances.

The only time my dad ever said anything about it in front of me, he just shook his head. "I hope they don't give him one too many second chances to hurt one of them real bad." Dad had seen a lot of family troubles in his work, and he didn't like the idea of always just letting things go.

Still, we protected Joel. We helped him fix his bike and hide his bruises. His mother was enough afraid of his dad that if she found out about what happened to Joel she would probably feel she had to tell his father. And then Joel would be in real trouble.

Of course, the East Side bullies would be in trouble too. And that would be OK, except we didn't want to be known as tattletales, and we sure didn't want Mr. McBride to actually hurt somebody. If he happened to be drunk when he heard that some older kids had hassled his boy, who knew what might happen?

"So, what are we gonna do today?" Kate asked as we assembled in the coal bin.

"We've got lots of business to cover," I said. "You don't have to stay if you don't want to."

"I'll stay," she said, but she was already looking all around the room, probably wondering why Joel wasn't looking at her as usual, and rocking in her chair.

Good, I thought. *She's already bored.*

I called the meeting to order slowly and formally and said we had many items to discuss.

"What's that mean?" Kate asked.

"Lots of stuff to talk about," I explained.

"Like what?"

"Oh, rules and regulations. Cases. Dues. A picnic."

"We're gonna have a picnic?"

"We might. We'll invite all the families of members and have some fun."

"Yea!" she said.

I didn't like her new interest, so I said, "First let's talk about club rules. Who can speak when and how we vote on things."

"We never vote on things," Jonathan said. "We just decide what sounds good, and we all nod." But as he was saying that, it was as if a light came on in his head and he realized I was just stalling. "But I think it would be a good idea," he said quickly. "I say you can't speak if you don't raise your hand.

And when you're called on by the captain, you have to say something good. You can't say something bad."

Kate looked as if she was in pain. "Who cares about this?" she whined. "Let's do something! Anyway, why do we have to have this dumb meeting today when we're gonna have another one tomorrow?"

"Back to this discussion about talking," Daniel said, looking thoughtful.

"Yeah," Jonathan said, "did Kate raise her hand?"

"Did you?" Thomas asked.

"I'm out of here," Kate said.

"Oh, really?" Jonathan said. "Do you have to go? We were going to talk about bylaws and maybe a constitution."

"Yuck!" she said, and Kate left.

It was all we could do to keep from cheering. In a way I hated to push her out like that, but there weren't going to be many cases where we could include her. This sure wasn't one of them, and we didn't know if we could trust her not to tell our secrets.

Finally we could get the rest of the details from Joel. Of course I had filled everyone in on as much as I knew when I'd invited them to the meeting. Reactions ranged from wanting revenge to fear. I was most surprised when Thomas finally spoke up and said what I had been thinking.

"This is a hard one," he said. "Living where I live, my first thought is to smash somebody. Get a gang together, wait for those guys to hassle somebody again, and make them regret it."

"Yeah!" Big Dan said. "Let's do it!"

"But that can't be what we should do," Thomas said. "It might make us all feel better for a little while, but then what? We would hurt some guys. Nothing good would come of it."

"Except maybe they'd leave me alone," Joel said.

"Well, OK, that would be good. But what happens when

they start telling their side of the story and they get a bigger bunch of guys together and come after us?"

"You've got the whole Lake Farm behind you, Thomas," Red Jon said. "Who could beat that?"

Thomas shook his head. "That would be a mess," he said. "A real mess. I can't think that's what God would want us to do."

We all sat there looking at Thomas, and I suppose most of the others felt the way I did—I wished I'd said that.

I nodded. "The Bible does say that we're supposed to love our enemies and pray for those who treat us bad."

"Wow," Jonathan said, shaking his head. "That sounds a lot better when one of your friends hasn't just been threatened."

"What are we gonna do?" Big Dan asked. "Tell 'em we love 'em and we're praying for 'em?"

"Only if it's true," Thomas said.

"Well, it's not," Jonathan said. "Maybe it's the right thing to do, but it's not what I'm feeling, and so I can't pretend it is."

It was strange to hear Jonathan so serious. Any second I thought I'd see that silly grin of his, but he was not kidding.

Joel was the same. "You don't know what it feels like to be surrounded and wonder if you're gonna be hurt. Who knew what they might do to me?"

"I know," Thomas said. "It would feel good to put them in their place, but what are we really *supposed* to do?"

"As junior deputies?" I asked.

"As Christians," Thomas said. "I don't see how we can all go to church and pray and read our Bibles and then just act like everybody else."

"Nobody's arguing with you," Daniel said. "But I don't feel loving toward those guys, and I don't feel like praying for them. I'd pray for the wrong thing."

"Like what?" Jonathan said.

"That they would get hurt. Who do they think they are?"

"I'm not excusing them," Thomas said. "But we can't expect them to be nice. Why should they be? They're just like everybody is starting to be nowadays. All they care about is themselves."

"But what about their threats against the Junior Deputies?" I said.

"They obviously have a plan," Thomas said. "I don't know who's next, but if they can read, they know who we are. They're obviously from the East Side, so they're probably starting with Joel, Jon, and Dan."

"That makes me feel great," Daniel said, his dark eyes narrow. "I'd like to think you guys would be watching out for us, ready to back us up and help us defend ourselves. What do you want us to do—pray for them when they chase us? Tell them we love them?"

This was not going the way I had planned. I had to admit I was hoping we'd come up with a plan of attack. We couldn't take this sitting down.

No one said anything until Thomas finally spoke again. "Sort of."

"Sort of what?" Daniel said.

"Well, if you can't tell them you love them, and you can't say you're praying for them, because you're not, tell them that the Junior Deputies are praying for them."

"Are we?"

"I will," Thomas said.

"Me too," I said, not sure I would have said that if Thomas hadn't.

"Man, oh, man," Joel said. "You guys sound like sissies. I don't think Jesus was a sissy."

"He's the one who said to love your enemies," Thomas said. "He's the one who asked God to even forgive the ones who put Him on the cross."

"Well, I'm not Jesus," Daniel said. "I don't think I want

God to forgive those bullies unless they admit they're wrong and ask for forgiveness."

"The people Jesus forgave didn't ask for it," Thomas said.

Daniel was mad now. He glared at Thomas. "When did you become so goody-goody? I mean, we're all Christians, but you've always been the tough guy. I don't want to be nasty to anyone, but I don't want some bullies scaring us and us just going around blessing them."

"I know it sounds weird," Thomas said. "But we're not supposed to be like everybody else."

"So if I'm next," Daniel said, "what am I supposed to do? Tell them you're praying for them and that at least some of us love them?"

"Just tell them the truth," Thomas said. "Tell them that we're not going to try to get back at them. Ask them what their problem is."

"What are they going to say?" Daniel asked. "That they're jealous? We know they are, but they're not going to say that."

"Tell them that no matter what they do," Thomas said, "we aren't going to take them on. Nothing they can do can make us hate them, so they might as well lay off. If they don't get the reaction they want, they'll get tired of bugging us."

"What if they don't?"

"Doesn't make any difference. We still have to do the right thing because it's the right thing."

Daniel and Jonathan sat shaking their heads.

I felt I needed to say something. We were falling apart. "I understand what you're saying, Thomas. But aren't we going to look like cowards? What kind of junior deputies are we if we let bullies hassle us?"

Thomas stood. "I'm not trying to sound like a preacher or better than you guys or anything, but if we can't pray for those kids like we're supposed to, maybe we should pray for ourselves. I know I'm the last one to start talking like a Sunday school teacher, but isn't it time we started growing up? Does being Christians mean anything in real life, or is it all just a bunch of stories and things we do on Sundays?"

The rest of us looked at the floor. How could you argue with Thomas? The problem was, we knew someone would be next and that it would probably be soon. Would it be Dan or Jon? And how would they react?

I had said I would pray for the bullies. It wouldn't be easy, but I had to keep my word. I knew Thomas would be doing the same thing. Neither of us knew it would become harder than ever within the next two days.

The Attack

Though I couldn't find anything in the Bible about God's sense of humor, all of us junior deputies thought it was funny Sunday when the pastor spoke on loving your enemies. He explained what it means to be "spitefully used." He said that is when people treat you badly because they hate you for some reason.

Thomas said he thought that the pastor's speaking on that very topic when we needed it most was more of an example of God's sense of timing than His sense of humor. Either way, I wished I'd had the nerve to ask the pastor what it really meant; what were we supposed to do when we were being attacked? It was sure easier to talk about this stuff than to do it every day.

That afternoon, just to keep Kate happy, we ran around the house and played in the yard rather than just meeting. Then, while she was busy with something else, we boys got together to remind each other what we would do if we were next in line for hassle from the East Side bullies.

Thomas was still pretty sure that Jonathan or Daniel would be next, because they went to the same school as Joel. "The bullies might be working their way up to the top," Thomas said, looking at me.

"Oh, great," I said. "I get to worry longer."

The rest of the guys figured Thomas was right, and they finally agreed that they would not fight back, at least for now.

"We can't win anyway," Jonathan said, "if the rest of you aren't there to help us. It still seems stupid to me to be left on our own, but I'll try the 'praying for you' and 'loving you' business."

"Not me," Daniel said. "I'll try telling them that they can't make enemies out of us unless they want to, but I can't guarantee I won't try smashing somebody in the face if they hit me first."

"What about turning the other cheek?" Thomas said. "Jesus says if somebody hits us we should turn the other cheek to them."

"And let them smack that one too?" Daniel said, as if he'd never heard that idea before. We knew he had. "Uh-uh, not me."

"Is that what you would do?" I asked Thomas. It just didn't sound like him.

"I don't know," he said, looking off in the distance. "I sure hope so." Then he chuckled, something he didn't often do.

"What's funny?" I asked.

"I guess I'm just hoping you or somebody else gets attacked when I'm there, because I don't think I have to turn the other cheek then. I can defend somebody else without feeling bad about it."

The next afternoon I caught up with Thomas as we were heading out of the school building.

He looked as if he was thinking. "I'm just wondering if they'll strike today," he said. "And whether it'll be Jonathan or Daniel."

"Are you sure you gave Jon and Dan the right advice?"

"Oh, I know it's the right thing to do. But I don't even know if *I'd* be able to do it."

"I'm pretty sure Daniel is not ready to do anything but fight."

"I know," Thomas said. "I just hope Jonathan doesn't try fighting. He'll get killed."

I told Thomas I would see him the next day. He headed south with a bunch of other Lake Farmers, and I headed west toward my house. I don't know why, but everything seemed to spook me.

I saw the pretty Mexican girl from my class. I sometimes liked to walk her to her house when none of my friends were looking. I wasn't supposed to be interested in girls, but Yolanda was something.

While I was walking with her, I saw a big dark-haired kid with a black jacket riding his bike slowly behind us. There didn't seem to be anyone else with him, but what if he was one of those guys? What if the others were hiding? What if he was a decoy? I kept peeking behind us, and my heart was pounding.

What were the bullies doing here? Would they try something with Yolanda around? Was I using her to keep myself safe? When we got to her street, I stopped and told her that I was in kind of a hurry and wouldn't be walking her all the way to her house. She seemed puzzled, but I didn't want to fall behind the group of kids walking my way. I sure didn't want Yolanda to get in the middle of anything.

As I turned, I noticed that the kid on the bike had stopped about thirty feet behind us and was just watching. "Oh, Yolanda," I said, as she skipped across the street. "Could I ask you something?"

She turned and came back.

I said quietly, "Don't look now, but do you see the kid on the bike behind me?"

She casually peeked over my shoulder and grinned. She nodded.

"Do you recognize him?"

"Yes."

"You do?"

"Yes."

"Does he go to Estes Junior High on the East Side?"

"No."

"Are you sure?"

"I ought to be."

"Who is he?"

"My brother."

Boy, was I relieved! I didn't even know Yolanda had a brother. She told me he was shy and wouldn't want to meet me. That was all right with me.

I started jogging home.

I was about a block from my house when I heard a bunch of kids yelling and saw them running back toward school. "What's going on?" I hollered.

"Fight!"

"Lake Farmers!"

I didn't want to hear that. It used to be that every time there was a fight it was either Lake Farmers against Lake Farmers or Lake Farmers against someone else. Parents were complaining that all the violence was coming from Lake Farm and they wanted those kids to go to school somewhere else. Somehow it had all quieted down, and there hadn't been more than a few fights during the school year, and only a couple of those involved Lake Farmers.

I ran three blocks, forgetting that I had already run that far from Yolanda's street. By the time I got to the scene I was so winded I could hardly breathe. I looked for Thomas in the crowd, because I knew he wasn't a fighter anymore.

Everywhere I looked there were Lake Farmers. But most of them were younger elementary school kids. They looked mad and excited, but they weren't fighting. They were watching. I pushed my way through the crowd and panicked when I realized what I was seeing.

Lying on the ground at the edge of the street was Thomas Christian, and towering over him were three older kids wearing Estes Junior High jackets. I knew immediately they were the East Side bullies Joel had described.

Thomas had rolled up into a ball, his knees at his chest, his hands clasped around his shins, his head tucked under. The three bullies were kicking him and yelling. "What'sa matter, big junior deputy hero? Why don't you arrest us?"

"Fight 'em! Kill 'em! C'mon, Tom, you can take 'em!" the younger Lake Farmers hollered.

One of the bullies kicked Thomas on top of the head, and Thomas buried his head in his arms.

I heard his muffled shouts. "I've got nothing against you guys. What's the problem? You're not going to make me fight you or hate you!"

Another bully danced around like a chicken and clucked. "Chicken, chicken, chicken!" he yelled.

I knew the bullies wouldn't stay long, because any time a crowd of students gathered to watch a fight, teachers couldn't be too far behind. I wanted to do something—to protect Thomas, to fight the bullies—but no one dared. Worse, *I* didn't dare. I hated myself for it. I wouldn't have been lying there like Thomas, trying to reason with them. But I also knew I wouldn't be fighting back, not from the way I was frozen in fear now.

But I had to try something. I grabbed a couple of young Lake Farmers by their collars and whispered into their ears. "Are these those guys' bikes?" I asked, pointing to three bikes lying on the grass.

"Yeah," they said.

"Get somebody else to help you and hide those bikes!"

"What?"

"*Now!* Do it! Just run them over to the parking lot and hide them between the cars!"

"What are you, crazy? They'll kill us!"

"They won't even see you. I'll keep them busy. Now go!"

But the two kids couldn't find anyone to help them. Each grabbed one bike and rolled it away.

I was still disgusted with myself for not jumping in and defending Thomas. I wanted to tell the bullies that their bikes were being stolen, but then they would beat up the kids I had told to do it. I had to wait until the bikes were hidden.

And there was still one bike left. I didn't know what else to do, so I shouted, "Cops!" and the bullies quickly looked for their bikes.

I grabbed the last one lying there and ran it toward the parking lot.

The biggest bully chased me, swearing and demanding I give him his bike.

I couldn't believe how fast he was. He ran me down quickly and shoved me into a parked car. I felt my ribs bang into the rear end of it and knew I would have a deep bruise. I let the bike go flying, and the kid jumped on it and started to ride off. The other two were looking frantically for theirs, while they were jeered at and threatened by the younger Lake Farmers.

The bully who had shoved me caught sight of the other two bikes and pointed them out to his friends. Soon all three were pedaling away to the laughs and shouts and pointed fingers of the crowd. No police were coming, and no one saw any teachers either.

"Who *were* those guys?" someone asked.

"Why didn't Tom Christian fight 'em?"

"He's chicken, a sissy. He doesn't fight anymore."

I was sick just hearing it. I knew Thomas was as strong and as tough as any one of those bullies, and I wanted to ask the kids saying that stuff why they hadn't helped him. But I hadn't helped him either.

Sure, I distracted them by making them think the police were coming, and I tried to hide the bikes, but why had I been so scared? I should have jumped on them, taken some of the beating myself. Or I should at least have said something like Thomas said, something to make them think and realize that they weren't going to get anywhere by attacking us.

But I had just stood there. Now Thomas's reputation was going to suffer. It would get all around the school that he had let three guys beat him and kick him. The crowd started to drift away. I didn't even want to face Thomas, but I knew I had to.

I found his books and put them in my backpack, then helped him to the sidewalk where he sat gasping for breath. "I had no idea you'd be next," I said.

"Me either," he said. And I had never seen him look so bad. His forehead was red and scratched. He had a nick cut out of his cheek. His jacket was torn, his pants dirty, his hair mussed. His hands had flecks of blood on them and scrapes on the backs.

"I can identify those guys," I said. "I'll tell my dad and that will be the end of it. You had twenty witnesses."

"No way," he said. "I had twenty people who saw me let them beat me up, and now they're going to find out I told on them? No. Promise me you won't do that, Toby. We have to fight our own battles."

"But you weren't fighting."

"Neither were you," he said.

I could have crawled in a hole. "I feel awful about that. I don't know what was the matter with me. *You* would have defended *me.*"

"Your deal with the bikes was pretty good," he said.

I didn't know why he was being so nice to me when I had let him down.

"I don't think they recognized you. Did they say anything?"

I shook my head. "I should have done more."

Then the assistant principal of our school hurried up. "Christian, you been fighting again? I thought you gave that up."

"I wasn't fighting, Mr. James," Thomas said. "I'm all right."

"There wasn't a fight going on over here just now?"

"No, sir, not exactly."

"Andrews, was there? What did you see?"

I hesitated. "There were some guys giving Thomas a bad time, but they weren't from our school."

"That right, Christian?"

Thomas nodded. "I didn't fight 'em. It's all over."

"Tell me who they are, and I'll call their school and have them dealt with," Mr. James said.

"Don't know their names," Thomas said. "Let's just drop it."

Mr. James shrugged. "It's none of my business if you don't want to do anything about it. You all right?"

"Yeah. I'll be fine."

I walked Thomas to the driveway that led to the Lake Farm Home and then handed him his books. "I said the right things when those guys were kicking me," he said, "but I wasn't thinking the right things."

"Were you thinking what I was thinking?"

"If you were thinking you'd like to tear them to pieces, I was," he said.

I nodded. "Except I was chicken. They called you chicken, but you were being brave."

"I didn't feel brave."

"But you were doing the right thing, Thomas. I would have been crying. And I probably would have tried to get away."

"Is that what you think I should have done, Toby?"

"I don't know. All I know is, I let you down."

"Well, I wasn't going to run away or look weak."

"Your friends thought you looked weak," I said.

"Did you?"

"'Course not. But those younger Lake Farmers did."

"Somebody's got to show them that you don't have to fight to win."

"You won? You think those bullies think you won?"

"They know *they* didn't win. They didn't get me to cry or run or beg."

"If they come after me, Thomas, I have no idea what I'll do. After today, I'm pretty sure I'll cave in."

"We've got to get to know those guys," Thomas said. "We can't understand them if we don't know them."

"You're out of your mind," I said.

Waiting

We couldn't know when the East Side bullies would strike again. Nothing happened the rest of that week, and some of the guys thought we should tell my dad what was going on. Thomas was dead set against that, and I agreed.

But I felt so bad about acting like a coward that I wondered if I even deserved to be a junior deputy, let alone captain.

Joel said he knew how I felt. "I was scared to death when they were hasslin' me."

"Yeah," I said, "but you talked back to them."

"Well, you made them run off."

"Yeah, I'm real brave."

"You're too hard on yourself," Thomas said. "You don't know what you'll do until it happens. I was so mad and embarrassed about rolling around on the ground in front of the other Lake Farmers that I thought I might jump up and kill somebody."

“You should have,” Big Dan said. “This is no game anymore. I’ve had enough, and I haven’t even seen these guys.”

“We’ve got to find out who they are, what their problem is, and see if we can get to them,” Thomas said.

“Get to them how?” Jonathan said. “If you say they’ve got reasons to be so mean, I don’t buy it. My dad says people who blame other people for the way they act are just copping out. He says you can’t blame where you live or how you live for the way you behave.”

“I know that’s true,” Daniel said. “There’s a guy in my neighborhood in jail for stealing and selling drugs, and his family is saying all the time that it’s because of the system and the environment. But my family lives on the same block in the same neighborhood, and we live in the same system. And we’re not criminals, and neither are most of the people we know.”

“I’m not saying they’ve got a right or even a good reason for what they’re doing,” Thomas said. “But we don’t know for sure what their problem is with us. What did we do to them?”

“Both times they used the name of our club and called us heroes and all that,” Joel said. “You know they’ve got to be jealous.”

“Probably,” Thomas said, “but how are we going to prove to them that being a junior deputy is a good thing? We help people. We’re not doing this to be famous.”

“Now you’re gonna want to get them into our club?” Jonathan said, looking amazed. “No way. They come in, I go out.”

“I don’t want them to be junior deputies,” Thomas said. “But maybe they need us. Maybe we can do something for them so they’ll see that we’re all right.”

Daniel was mad. “Why are you so worried about convincing them that we’re good guys? They should know that!

We're not the ones going around scaring people, threatening them, beating them up."

"But if we did something for them," Thomas said, "if we helped them or solved something for them, they wouldn't have any reason not to like us."

"They don't have a reason now," Jonathan said. "Man, you have really lost it. They almost knock you unconscious, and you still want to be kind to them."

I wasn't saying much. I knew everyone else knew by now that I had not come through when Thomas needed me. That hurt. A couple of the guys tried to compliment me on getting the bikes out of there, but that didn't change anything. I was still miserable. I had gotten a look at what I was really like inside, and I didn't like what I saw.

"It wouldn't hurt us to be kind to them," Thomas said. "We'll be the stronger ones. It doesn't take a man to beat up somebody, especially when your friends are with you. I want to know who these guys are. I think one of 'em plays basketball at Estes."

"Two of 'em do," Joel said. "At least they used to. That's how I knew they were from Estes."

"Maybe Toby and I will go over there sometime and see who knows them and can tell us something about them."

"Me?" I said.

"Who else?" Thomas said.

"How about someone who goes to school over that way?"

"You're still scared of them?"

That was exactly right, but there was no way I was about to admit it.

"When are we supposed to do this?" I said.

"Next time I'm at your place during the week. We can go there right after school."

I didn't like the idea, but everyone else did. It wasn't that they agreed with Thomas any more than I did. But they liked the idea that if I was involved, they wouldn't have to be.

The only problem was, even though my parents arranged to have Thomas come home with me the following Wednesday after school and to stay until school was out Thursday, the East Side bullies weren't using our schedule.

Thomas didn't know anybody at Estes, because all the Lake Farmers went to school in our neighborhood. But I had a cousin and a couple of other friends there, and so that's where we started.

My cousin knew immediately who we were talking about and told us their names. "They terrorize this whole school," he said. "Everybody knows them. We call them the Leathers, because they like to wear leather jackets."

"And two of them are basketball players?"

"They were. They quit. Well, one of them quit when the other one was kicked off the team."

"For what?"

"I don't know. Rumor was that he was on drugs, but I think he was just rebellious. Couldn't be coached. Both of those guys were good players, and when the coach dumped one and lost the other, we were a worse team."

"Are these poor kids?" Thomas asked. "They don't have the kinds of things everybody else has?"

"Are you kidding?" my cousin said. "These are rich kids. They have everything they want. And they get away with everything at school. You should hear the things they get away with saying to the teachers."

"Why don't they get in trouble?"

"One of 'em's dad is on the school board. I don't know if that makes any difference, but there has to be some reason they get away with so much."

"So where are they?" Thomas asked, looking around.

"They went riding out of here early today," my cousin said. "They convinced the last period study hall teacher that they had to go."

Thomas and I looked at each other. I knew we were thinking the same thing. We were just hoping they weren't up to something again right then. We rode to Daniel's house.

Daniel said he had seen Jonathan after school and that everything was OK then.

We called Joel and asked if he could join us at Jonathan's house.

"I just called there," he said. "Jonathan's mom said he wasn't home yet. She was worried about him."

"Call back and tell her we'll find him. Then meet us at the park."

At the park, the Junior Deputies, except for Jonathan and Kate, of course, stood straddling our bikes and trying to figure out which way Jonathan would have walked home. Then we started riding that way.

We didn't see anything at first, but then I found Jonathan's notebook in the street. Was he leaving a trail on purpose, the way Hansel and Gretel left bread crumbs? Or had he just dropped his notebook by mistake?

We found another book of his near some shrubbery at the edge of a sidewalk.

Thomas and I got off our bikes and shouldered through there. Sure enough, Jonathan's backpack was on the ground. We called out for him and heard a groan.

"In here, guys!" I yelled.

The others came in on their bikes.

There was Jonathan, sitting in some bushes. His shoes were gone, and his jacket had been taken too.

"The bullies?" I asked.

He nodded, crying. "My mom will kill me if I show up at home without my shoes and jacket."

"Did they hurt you?" Thomas said.

He nodded, turning and lifting his shirt to show bruises on his back.

“We have to change plans,” Thomas said. “Now we have to tell somebody. This has gone far enough.”

“No!” Jonathan’s face was almost as red as his hair. Then he said, “I don’t think they took my stuff. They just ripped it off me and threw it somewhere. Help me find it.”

We dug through the bushes and tall grass until we found his jacket and one shoe.

“I’ll stay here all night till I find the other one,” Jonathan said. “If I show up at home dressed anything different than the way I left this morning, I’m dead meat.”

“Your mom’s not that way,” I said.

“I know,” he said. “She won’t hurt me or anything. But she’ll drag everything out of me. As it is, I don’t know how to explain why I’m so late. I won’t lie to her, but I don’t want to tell her about those guys either.”

We told him to just tell her the truth—that some bigger kids were bugging him and that he had to find his shoes and his jacket before he could go home. Maybe it wouldn’t sound as serious to her as it really was. If she asked who they were, he could just say he didn’t want to get them into trouble.

“What did they say?” Thomas asked.

“Same stuff they said to you and Joel. That I thought I was somebody special just because I was a pretend deputy. They said, ‘Deputy this!’ when they took my jacket and ran into the bushes with it. Then they pulled off my shoes, and they threw them over the trees.”

“Over those trees?” I said, pointing at the tall trees beyond the sidewalk.

He nodded.

“Then we didn’t look far enough for the other one.”

We picked around till we found his other shoe.

Jonathan was really relieved and said he’d better get going.

Thomas wanted to know something first, though. “What did you say to them?”

"Well, I felt like an idiot," Jonathan said, "but I told them what you said to tell them. I told them that some of the Junior Deputies were praying for them and that nothing they did to us would make us not like them."

"Good for you," Thomas said.

"I can't say I really meant it," Jonathan said. "I don't like them very much right now."

"What did they say when you said that?" Daniel asked.

"They laughed. They said, 'You'll hate us soon enough. When we get through with you and your friends, you'll hate us plenty.'"

Jonathan ran off toward home.

We followed him from a distance, because he was afraid the bullies would come back.

They didn't, at least not then. But it wouldn't be long. I had a feeling I would be next, and I wasn't looking forward to it.

Telling It All

That night after dinner, while Thomas was at our house, Mrs. Bynum called my dad. Then Dad asked Thomas and me if he could talk with us.

"What do you know about this business with Jonathan today?" he asked.

"Not much," I said, feeling like I was lying. But I didn't really know much. I hadn't seen it happen. I had gotten only Jonathan's side of the story. But I knew more than I was saying, and that made me feel bad.

"How about you, Thomas?" Dad said.

Thomas looked down, then told him the story of our finding Jonathan in the bushes.

"Did they hurt him?"

"No, sir. I mean, not much."

"Do you think it was serious, or just kids being kids?"

Thomas hesitated, and I knew he would not lie to my dad. He didn't want to tell Dad everything, that he had also been a victim, and so had Joel. But he couldn't say this wasn't serious. "We heard these were some tough guys at the junior high, but we'd rather just handle it."

"You don't want me to get involved, find out the names, send a car to the school and put a stop to it?"

"No, sir," Thomas said quickly. "We'll let you know if it's something we can't handle."

"I don't want you fighting these guys."

"We don't want to either, Dad," I said. "Thomas really thinks we should try a whole different thing."

"Like what?"

Thomas told my dad his idea about telling them we're praying for them and that nothing they did would make us hate them. I could see that sounded a little strange to Dad. It had to make him wonder if there wasn't more happening here than we were saying.

"That's a good approach," he said. "But don't expect it to get you too far."

"I've been meaning to ask you about that, Mr. Andrews," Thomas said. "If that's what we're supposed to do, if that's what Jesus would do, how come it doesn't work?"

"Well, a soft answer is supposed to turn away wrath. Usually."

Thomas looked at me, reminding me of when he spoke kindly to the Leathers while they were kicking him.

"It doesn't always work, though, does it?" I said.

"Not always," Dad said. "And the people who don't calm down from a kind word are the same ones who will just be more frustrated when you tell them you love them or are praying for them. Some people just need to be stopped and disciplined."

"Well, that's what we'd like to do," Thomas said. "But we're trying to do the right thing. It's not easy. I mean, it's not going to be easy."

Dad was studying us, and it made me wonder if we were going to have to tell him the whole truth: that the East Side bullies, the Leathers, were after the Junior Deputies for some reason.

I knew that would bring out the best, or the worst, in my dad, and he would want to defend us. We just couldn't let that happen unless we had to. Instead of looking like real junior deputies, we would look like little kids who ran to their parents or tattled on people.

By the time we were through answering Dad's questions, I knew he knew more than he was letting on. He could see what was going on, even if he didn't know all the details. He didn't know that more of us had been attacked, but he sure knew there was more to this than Jonathan Bynum getting his stuff tossed around.

Dad called Mrs. Bynum back and told her to be sure and call him if Jonathan had any more trouble with the boys. Then he told us that he expected us to know when we should tell him and when we should try to handle this ourselves.

We told him we would be careful.

Later, in my room, I told Thomas I felt guilty.

"Why?"

"I don't know. I guess I just feel like if I don't tell my dad everything, I'm lying. If we're trying to do the right thing by talking nice to these bullies, I shouldn't be lying to my dad."

"You're not lying."

"But isn't keeping things from him the same as deceiving?"

"If you think so, then tell him. If I thought so, I'd tell him."

And I knew Thomas would. He was being so careful about this whole thing that I wondered what had happened to him. I knew he was a Christian when I first met him, but now he seemed so serious about it that he was making the rest of us nervous. Maybe that was what made me feel as if I should say more to my dad.

"Why are you like this?" I asked Thomas.

"I don't know," he said. "I've been thinking about it for a long time. It seems like we always read these Bible stories and memorize verses and pray about living for God. And then we don't really do it. We care about ourselves. We want revenge. We talk about people. It just doesn't make sense."

That was all I needed to hear. "I'm going to tell my dad everything," I said, rolling out of bed.

"Are you sure?"

"What did you just say?" I said. "The Bible says we're supposed to honor our father and mother. I don't think I'm honoring my dad by keeping stuff from him."

"Well, could you at least tell him we still want to handle it ourselves?"

I had to think about that one. "I'll ask him," I said. "But you know my dad."

"I know. That's why you may need to beg."

"Begging doesn't work so well with him."

"I really don't want him to rescue us," Thomas said.

"I know," I said. "If you did, you wouldn't have let those guys knock you down and kick you."

"That makes me want even more to settle this ourselves."

"You want to get back at them."

"No! I want to win them over somehow."

"I think you're dreaming," I said.

"I know you do. And so does your dad. And if you tell him everything, he's not going to let me try."

"You might be surprised," I said. "But what you're doing is following your conscience, right?"

"Right."

"Then shouldn't I follow mine?"

"I guess," Thomas said, "as long as this is bothering you because of what you know is right and not because you've just got a bad feeling."

"My conscience is just as Christian as yours," I said.

Thomas looked at me funny, like I had just said the

dumbest thing he'd ever heard. "I wasn't saying it wasn't," he said. "I'm still against this, but do what you've got to do."

I decided to think about it and pray about it some more, but that didn't last long. The longer I lay there keeping the whole truth from my dad, the worse I felt. Was God making me feel bad about this?

What was the worst thing that could happen if I told Dad? Well, he could tell us to stay out of it, to back off, to let him handle it. That would be bad, because then the Junior Deputies would look like just a bunch of babies.

The best that could happen? Dad could offer a little advice and let us take care of our own business. He would always be there for backup, of course.

I didn't care anymore. I wanted it to go the way Thomas wanted it, of course, but I couldn't go on keeping information from my dad just to make that happen. I had to take my chances. I padded downstairs where Dad was just turning off the news.

"You should be asleep," he said.

"I know." And then I let it all spill out, everything. Even how the East Side bullies had beat up Thomas and I had tried to help but felt like a chicken.

Dad sighed. "Thanks for telling me," he said, "but I hope you don't expect me to fight your battles for you. There comes a time when you have to stand up for yourself. I can't be bailing you out all the time."

I was so relieved I could hardly believe it. I said, "To tell you the truth, Dad—"

"Finally," he said, smiling.

"—I was afraid you were going to make me stay out of it and let you take care of it."

He shook his head. "Time to grow up, pal. You know I'll be there when you need me, and if these guys really hurt anybody or steal anything or break the law some other way, we'll have to deal with it. Meanwhile, I like the way you guys are going about it. I'm impressed that Thomas is so concerned about doing the right thing, but don't forget that these guys don't play by your rules."

Thomas was happy about the way that turned out. "I have to admit you made the right decision—telling your dad," he said. "Let's hope we don't have to get him into this."

"Of course, now he'll be asking what's going on every day."

"That's all right," Thomas said. "Maybe he'll have some advice. Meanwhile, we've got to figure Daniel will be next."

"Why?"

"Because I think they're working their way up to you, Toby."

"I thought so too, but they got to you out of order."

"Maybe they don't know I'm the lieutenant," Thomas said. "That newspaper story just said you were captain. It didn't say what ranks the rest of us were. The Leather bullies probably figure a Lake Farmer is just one of the guys. Daniel looks big enough to be your right-hand man."

Until we finally fell asleep, Thomas and I tried to think of ways to protect both Daniel and me. That wouldn't be easy, but it seemed important. I wasn't convinced that Daniel would be next.

"I'll stick with you," Thomas said. "But Jonathan and Joel are not going to be able to protect Daniel."

"Daniel might be able to protect himself!"

"That's what I'm afraid of," Thomas said, laughing. "He'll be outnumbered, and they're all stronger than he is, but it would be just like Daniel to try to take them all on."

"I don't think he's going to try the soft answer routine."

Thomas shook his head. "I wish he would."

"Dream on," I said.

The next day I saw Thomas on the way back to our classrooms after lunch.

"As long as I'm back at Lake Farm by five, I can make sure Daniel gets home," he said. "We get out earlier than they do, and they get out earlier than Estes, so we can walk over there in time to keep an eye on him. Joel and Jonathan can join us if they want to. Maybe if we're all there, those guys will pick another day to hassle Daniel."

Thomas's hunches were often right, but I didn't feel good about this one. I wanted to protect Daniel, of course, but I wasn't sure he would be the next target. Still, it wouldn't hurt to make sure Daniel was OK. I think Thomas was really thinking that he could keep Daniel from doing something stupid, like trying to fight those guys himself. Maybe Thomas thought Daniel would even talk like a Christian if he knew Thomas was watching.

After school we hurried off toward Daniel's elementary school, telling Kate to tell Mom I'd be home by five.

"Where are you guys goin'?" she asked. "What are you doing? Can I come?"

"Not this time, Kate," I said.

"I'm a junior deputy too, you know."

"I know," I said. "Maybe next time."

Something didn't feel right, but I didn't know what it was. Only a few kids from the other elementary school would be walking toward us. Most of them lived the other direction, and we were alone on the sidewalk with about a half mile to walk. We would get to the elementary about the time they let out and about twenty minutes before Estes Junior High let out.

Of course, the Leathers had not let the time of day stand in their way before. Somehow they were able to get out early when they wanted to. Maybe they would be waiting to ambush Daniel. I knew he would be glad to see us. I would if I were in his place.

We took our last right turn, and the elementary school came into sight. But heading our way, about halfway between us and the school, came three big kids on bikes. They wore black jackets, and they were pedaling toward us for all they were worth.

We stopped and looked at each other and then back at them. A few seconds later we could see their faces, and we knew for sure. It was the East Side bullies, and Daniel was nowhere in sight.

They seemed as surprised to see us as we were to see them.

The Battle

"What do we do?" I whispered.

"Nothing," Thomas said. "Just stand here and see what they do."

"How'd they know we were coming?"

"They didn't," Thomas said. "They couldn't have. *I* didn't even know we were coming until today, and I didn't tell anybody. Who'd you tell?"

"Only Kate, just now."

"Then they're as surprised as we are."

The three leather-jacketed Estes junior highers raced straight toward us, then slammed on their brakes and skidded to a stop right in front of us.

I jumped back at the last minute, and Thomas stepped onto the grass just in case, which made the three of them laugh.

"Well, well, well," the biggest one said, "look who we have here. Where do you boys think you're going?"

"We're—" I began, before Thomas elbowed me.

"Where are *you* guys going?" Thomas asked.

"We don't answer to you, little boy," the bully said.

I had never heard anybody call Old Tom a little boy. He was easily as big as any one of these guys and probably stronger. They would have been afraid of him one-on-one.

Thomas had spoken softly, kindly. He continued without being sarcastic. "I don't see that we answer to you either."

The three traded glances and smiled. "You don't, huh? Soon enough, you will, unless you want some more of what we gave you the other day."

"Let's go, Toby," Thomas said and started to walk between the bikes. Two bullies moved their bikes together so we couldn't pass.

"Oh, it's Toby, is it? We couldn't tell for sure. I mean, we've only seen you in the paper where you're a big shot, showing off your badge."

I couldn't say anything. My face felt hot, and I knew I was red.

"You've seen him before," Thomas said.

I thought, *Oh, great. Thanks, Thomas. First you tell them who I am, and now you tell them they've seen me before.* And sure enough, he did.

"He made a fool of you when you were trying to finish me off. He's the reason you couldn't find your bikes."

"We found 'em," one said. "And now that we've got you two alone, we ought to finish the job we started."

"I can't let you do that," Thomas said.

"You can't let us?" the first bully repeated. "You had a whole gang of Lake Farmers with you last time, and they couldn't do anything."

"Come on," the third bully said. "We were savin' the captain here for last. Let's stick to the plan."

"Yeah," the first said, smiling. "We're sticking to our plan. Another day, another deputy. Anyway, we gotta hurry."

I had no clue what they meant.

Thomas looked puzzled too as they stepped back and started to move around us. Where were they headed? Daniel would be getting out of school about now, and they were going the wrong direction.

The biggest of the three stopped and turned to look back at us.

"Were you two looking for us today?" he asked.

"Like I said," Thomas said, still pleasant, "we don't answer to you any more than you answer to us."

With that the bully jumped off his bike and threw it to the ground.

I tensed, ready to run or fight or whatever.

The other two started to get off their bikes, but the first growled, "I'll handle this. Just keep an eye on the captain."

The junior higher rushed up to Thomas and stood nose to nose with him, little specks flying from his mouth as he spoke, making Thomas blink. "I said I wanted to know where you were going and whether you were looking for us!"

Thomas never took his eyes away from the bully's. "And I told you it was none of your business."

"Do I hafta beat you up again to make it my business?"

"You'd kill me before I'd tell you anything I don't want to tell you. Just like where you're going is none of our business unless you try to hassle our friends."

"Oh, so you've been getting the message, huh? Is that what you were going to do today? Protect one of your friends? Well, you guessed wrong. You're going the wrong way."

Thomas was speechless. Finally he said, "You know, I don't know what you guys' problem is with us. We've never done anything to you. We don't even know you. Maybe if we got to know each other, we'd like one another. Ever think of that?"

"Like we'd want to get to know you!"

"How would you know?"

"Ryan, we gotta go, or we're gonna be late," one said.

Ryan turned on his friend. "No names, you idiot!"

"Oh, I know who you are," Thomas said. "You played basketball last year. We ought to shoot some hoops together someday."

Ryan whirled back to face Thomas, looking as if he didn't know what to say. "How do you know us?" he demanded.

"How do you know *us?"* Thomas asked.

"You creeps are in the paper every other day, thinkin' you're hot stuff."

"You guys are legends at your school," Thomas said, "but maybe if you were nice guys instead of bullying everybody, you'd get in the paper too. The school board would be proud of you."

Ryan shot a look at one of the other two, who looked stunned.

"Yeah, you," Thomas guessed, pointing at the boy. "You're Matt, right?"

"Don't tell 'im!" Ryan commanded, but Matt had already nodded.

"Your dad is on the school board, right?"

"Shut up!" Ryan said, getting back on his bike. "Let's get going." He looked at me. "We're saving the best until last."

"That makes you Andre, right?" Thomas said, pointing to the third bully, the one who hadn't spoken yet.

"Let's go!" Ryan shouted, and they all pedaled off.

I couldn't believe I wasn't shaking, the way I felt inside. We stood and watched them, and I said, "I can't believe you remembered those names."

"I had to take a chance," Thomas said. "When the one guy called the other one Ryan, it reminded me what your cousin said."

"My cousin wasn't sure himself."

"It was a gamble. I think it paid off. I think we spooked them."

"We? I probably would have done nothing again, just like last time."

"You made them look like idiots last time," Thomas said. "Don't forget that."

"Let's find the other deputies," I said. "Tell them they don't have to worry anymore, at least today."

As we walked on, Thomas said, "I wonder why those bullies think we've got another junior deputy at our school. They must know Daniel goes to school with Joel and Jonathan."

Kate!

We both stopped on the sidewalk. "We do have another junior deputy at our school!" I said.

And we turned to run back the way we had come.

With our backpacks swinging and banging against us, we cut corners and ran through yards, but the East Side bullies were still too far ahead of us to even see. Would Kate be home by now? Probably not. She often took her time and talked with her friends.

I was gasping and could hear Thomas sucking in air too. My chest hurt, and my heart raced, but I couldn't stop, couldn't slow down, couldn't rest. "You gonna try to sweet-talk 'em again?" I managed as we sprinted.

"Not if they're hurtin' somebody," he said.

"Good!" I shouted. I wasn't afraid anymore. Maybe I'd turn my own cheek if they smacked me, and maybe I admired Thomas and wished I could talk to them the way he did. But if they were thinking about hurting my sister, I'd never forgive myself if I didn't make them regret it.

We ran past our school, but instead of taking the usual route that Kate and I walked home, we ran on down Oakland Drive and came up Springmont Street so we would be facing her as she came toward the house.

I didn't think I could run another step as we turned onto

Springmont, but what I saw in the distance made me forget the pain. Kate was with four of her girlfriends, and they were all trying to skip out of the way as the three Leathers rode at them on their bikes.

The girls screamed and cried, but every time they tried to run away, another bully rode in front of them. As far as we could tell, none of the girls had been hit, but they all looked scared to death.

"Hey!" Thomas shouted, and I couldn't believe he could be that loud when he was so out of breath. "Hey! Leave them alone!"

But it was clear none of them heard him. Not the bullies or the girls. Now we both shouted as we ran, but still no one noticed us until we were almost upon them.

Two of Kate's friends broke free and ran away. The other two stood paralyzed on the sidewalk while the bullies forced Kate into the street. A passing car honked as the kids got too close. That was the last straw.

Thomas and I charged into the middle of the bullies, shouting and surprising them.

"Run home!" I told the other two girls. "Kate! Go home, right now!"

"Not so fast!" Ryan said. "Stay where you are. You go home when I say."

"She goes home now," Thomas said quietly. "Do what your brother says, Kate."

Kate was crying, and I was so mad I could have killed somebody. "Go on, Kate," I said. "You're safe now."

She turned and ran toward our house, about a block and a half away, but as soon as she took off, Ryan began to ride after her.

I froze, but Thomas started to chase them, bumping into me and making me move. As soon as I was moving, I ran faster than I ever had.

Ryan hadn't built up much speed yet, and I caught him

before he got to Kate. It looked like he was going to try to run her down. She looked back and squealed as I grabbed him from behind and lifted my feet off the ground. That almost doubled the weight on his bike and made it impossible for him to control it. He swayed right and left and finally tipped over with me on top of him.

Out of the corner of my eye I watched for Thomas to come and help me. No way I could take an eighth grader. But Thomas had Andre's arm in both hands and was talking into his ear. When Andre raced off on his bike, Thomas did the same to Matt, and then Matt rode off.

Ryan rolled away from his bike and flipped me over, getting me in a headlock and making it impossible for me to breathe. I elbowed him in the ribs, but he didn't let go for long. He was pulling back to slug me when Thomas bowled him over.

Ryan leaped to his feet as we both came at him. He stopped and held up his hands. "Two against one. No fair."

"No fair?" Thomas howled, laughing. "You three surround our junior deputies one at a time, and now you tell me two sixth graders against a big man like you is unfair."

"I'll get you in trouble with the school board, man," Ryan said, the veins in his neck bulging.

"Where are your friends now?" Thomas said.

"Going to get help," Ryan said. "You're in for it."

Thomas laughed. "I told 'em both Kate would have the county sheriff out here in a few minutes. They didn't stay long."

Ryan turned to me. "You're so chicken you'd tell your daddy?" he said.

"Not me," I said. "But Kate might."

"You guys leave me alone," Ryan said, moving toward his bike.

Thomas stood in front of him.

"Let me by," Ryan said, a quiver in his voice.

"Well, look who's afraid now," Thomas said.

"Two against one," Ryan said again. "No fair."

"You think it would be fair if it was just you and me?" Thomas said.

"I'd knock you out," Ryan said.

"We may have to see about that," Thomas said. "I know where you live. And someday I'm going to just show up to talk to you."

"I'll fight you anytime," Ryan said.

"Maybe you will," Thomas said. "But I don't know if I want to fight you. Maybe we'd be better friends than enemies, but if you hurt any more of my friends or even scare 'em, you're going to wish you hadn't."

Showdown

Thomas barely made it back to the Lake Farm Home before five o'clock, and I was left with a mess at my house. Kate seemed nearly crazy from fear, insisting that she never wanted to walk to or from school again. Her friends' parents began calling, confusing the bullies with "Kate's brother and his rowdy friends." Dad wouldn't be home for an hour, and I had to try to keep everybody cool.

Of course, Mom was not happy about what had happened. I wound up promising to stay with Kate to and from school every day until she wasn't scared anymore. I also had to convince Mom that this was a problem Dad knew about and that hc was letting the Junior Deputies handle it.

"No one got hurt," I said, "because we were there." I didn't say how close we had come to not being there.

In school the next day Thomas and I met at recess and planned our next move.

"Have your cousin find out where this Ryan lives," Thomas said. "If you have to walk Kate home every day, we can only see him on the weekend. If your parents sign me out of the Home for Friday night through Sunday afternoon, we can visit him on Saturday."

"*Visit* him?"

Thomas nodded. "We've got to talk to that kid alone. You could see he was scared when his friends weren't around."

That Saturday we rode over to the nice area in the park section where the expensive homes were. At the top of a hill we parked our bikes under some trees—Thomas was riding my big brother Jason's old one—and sat in the grass. From there we had a view of Ryan's huge house and lawn. It was early, and it looked like no one was up.

Within a half hour or so we began to hear and see things around the house that told us their day was starting. Lights came on, the dog was let out, Ryan's father put his golf bag in the trunk of his car and drove off. We heard Ryan shouting at his little sisters and his mother.

Pretty soon we realized how lucky we were. Ryan's mother told him to mow the lawn while she and the girls were gone. She told him she would be home by noon, and she kept telling him to get started on the yard before she left. He told her he would have it done by the time she got back, so not to worry about it.

We watched as Ryan's mother and his sisters drove off, the little girls in ballet outfits. Soon Ryan came out through the door at the side of the garage, carrying a gas can toward a small shed in the back yard.

"Perfect," Thomas said. "Let's go."

We left our bikes and scampered down the hill, crouching behind the big wood fence around Ryan's property. We waited until he went into the shed to get the lawn mower, then made our move.

"Are we trespassing?" I said.

"Well, we weren't invited," Thomas whispered, "but

we're visiting a guy we know. Anyway, we don't intend to hurt him or anything."

We were standing in the yard when Ryan backed out of the shed with the lawn mower.

"Good morning," I said.

He jumped and turned around, then turned pale. "What do you guys want?" he said. "My dad's right inside."

"You don't have to lie to us," Thomas said.

"I'm not lyin'! I'm gettin' the mower out for him because Matt and Andre are on their way over. You'd better not be here when they get here."

"We're not afraid of your friends or you, Ryan," I said. "You should know that by now."

"Yeah? Well, I'm not afraid of you either," Ryan said.

"Then relax," Thomas said. "We could tell you that our friends are behind the fence"—Ryan looked that way for a second—"but we'd be lying, just like you are. We just want to talk."

"What about?"

"About why you guys are hasslin' us. What's the deal? We haven't done anything to you. We didn't even fight back when you tried to beat up our guys, except when you tried to run down Toby's sister."

Ryan's eyes darted, and he seemed to be short of breath. "We don't like you guys, that's all."

"Because we were in the paper?" I said.

"Maybe. You guys think you're so cool, solving crimes and doing good for people, and all that."

"What's wrong with that?" Thomas said. "You have a problem with people doing good things?"

It was obvious Ryan didn't know what to say. He and his friends were bullies just because they wanted to be, and they were jealous of anybody who got attention for being good instead of bad. He ignored the question.

"Listen, are you guys gonna leave me alone, or am I going to have to get you in trouble?"

"How are you going to do that?" I asked. "Are you going to tell on us?"

"Maybe I will!"

"For what? What have we done?"

"You knocked me off my bike yesterday." He pointed at Thomas. "And he knocked me over when you already had me on the ground."

"You tried to run down my little sister," I said. "You think she's really a junior deputy? Somebody who can hurt you? You call yourself a man, picking on little girls? Did you really think we'd let you get away with that?"

"What are you gonna do about it?"

"We're going to do what we did yesterday. We're not going to let you run down her or her friends."

"So now this is payback time?" Ryan said, still looking scared.

"Look," Thomas said, "we're not going to do anything to you. We don't want to have to fight you."

"Because you couldn't win."

"We think we could win a fair fight. But we're tired of you ambushing us and ganging up on us."

"What do you call this?" Ryan said. "Aren't you ganging up on me?"

"How does it feel?" I asked.

"It feels all right. I'm not scared."

But he was, and it was obvious.

"If you beat me up," he continued, "you'll never get away with it. I know who you are, and you're on my property."

"We're not going to beat you up," Thomas said. "Can't you understand that? We want to have a truce, be friends, make you see that you don't have to be our enemy."

Ryan looked speechless. He didn't want to get beat up in

his own yard, but he seemed totally puzzled by what Thomas was saying.

"We're not bad guys," Thomas continued. "If you got to know us, you'd know that. We're not the kind of guys who deserve to get beat up."

"And I am?" Ryan said.

"Yes, you are," I said, hoping I wasn't messing up whatever Thomas was trying to do. "We could hurt you and probably not even get in trouble for it because everybody knows what you guys have been up to, terrorizing anybody smaller than you, ganging up on people, all that."

Ryan kept looking around as if he hoped someone would show up to save him. I'm sure he was having a hard time believing we weren't going to hurt him. Finally he said, "So you want a truce?"

"At least," Thomas said. "I suppose it would be too much to ask that you guys apologize."

"For what?"

"For what you did to Joel McBride, to me, to Jonathan Bynum, to Kate Andrews."

"We didn't hurt anybody. We were just playing."

"Yeah, sure," Thomas said. "So what about the truce?"

"You leave me alone, and I'll leave you alone," Ryan said quickly.

Thomas looked at me and then back at Ryan. He stuck out his hand. "Friends?" Thomas said.

Ryan ignored his hand. "A truce isn't between friends," he said. "It's between enemies."

"But we're not your enemies," Thomas said. "Why do we have to be enemies?"

"You want a truce or not?"

"Yeah, but—"

"Then you'd better take it," Ryan said. "It's all you're getting from me. I'm not interested in being friends with some sixth-grade orphan."

I shot a glance at Thomas, who looked hurt. What had been the point of that comment? I was mad and would have loved to pop Ryan right where he stood. But I wasn't sure Thomas would defend me if I started something. He was determined not to fight, especially when we outnumbered Ryan. He didn't want to be guilty of what the Leathers were guilty of.

"You know what?" I said. "I've seen both of you fight, and Thomas could take you. He may be younger, but he's just as big, and he's quicker and stronger."

"I already took *him,*" Ryan said. "We had him whimpering on the ground."

"Yeah," I said, "you and your coward friends."

Thomas interrupted. "We still want at least a truce," he said. "Are we gonna stop hassling each other?"

"We haven't hassled them, Thomas," I said. "I agree with trying to be nice, but let's don't pretend we've been doing what they've been doing."

"Yeah," Ryan said, "but you're hassling me now. You leave me alone, I'll leave you alone. That's the deal."

Thomas looked at me, I guess to see if I was going to mess things up again.

I shrugged.

"Deal," Thomas said, thrusting out his hand again.

Ryan ignored it again. "Now get out of my yard."

"Some truce," I said.

"We'll take what we can get," Thomas said.

Thomas and I didn't say anything to each other until we got all the way back to my house.

"I know you're mad at me," I said, "but you were letting him walk all over you. We had the drop on him. We could have taken him. He was scared—you could see it."

"Yeah, I saw it," Thomas said. "And I didn't like it very

much. He looked the way each of us feels when they have us surrounded. That's why it has to stop."

"Well, I'm sorry I couldn't go along with everything you were saying, but—"

"But nothing," Thomas said. And he was clearly mad now. "You almost had me fighting the guy, which was exactly what I don't want to do."

"But you could take him!"

"I know I could! We've been through this, Toby. I don't want this to get to where the Junior Deputies are fighting the East Side Leathers. That can't be the right thing; it can't be what we're supposed to do."

"Well, what *are* we supposed to do? He wasn't interested in a real truce or being friends or even seeing our side of it. He said whatever he had to to get rid of us and save his own skin."

"At least we got something out of it."

I was glad Thomas thought so, but I thought we had failed. Whatever we were trying to do—get Ryan to admit he had been wrong, to apologize, to become our friend—none of that happened. I didn't even know if we should believe we had a truce. All he said was that if we left him alone, he would leave us alone.

We found out later that day just how well we did in trying to make peace with Ryan, when my dad came looking for Thomas and me and said we had to talk. He took us up to my room and had us sit on the bed. "I need you to tell me everything that went on today," he said.

I told him every detail I could remember, and Thomas filled in the rest. Dad was angry, but I couldn't tell if it was at us or what. He seemed satisfied with our story, though, and even with Thomas's approach. "But you know, boys," he said, "sometimes you don't realize who you're dealing with."

"What do you mean?" I asked.

"Ryan's father is an attorney," Dad said. "And a good one. He even has friends who can get things done on the weekend. Look at this."

Dad showed us an official-looking document with all kinds of big words and long paragraphs. It was called a "restraining order."

"Usually these are used to keep husbands and wives away from each other when they're going through divorces and don't trust each other," Dad said. "This one is written to keep you two away from Ryan."

"You're kidding," Thomas said.

"I wish I was," Dad said. He read us the parts that restricted us from coming within 200 feet of Ryan and stated that we had trespassed on his property with the intention of threatening him with bodily harm.

"What's that mean?" I asked.

"It means," Dad said, "that if you have any more contact with Ryan, you've violated a court order."

"Then how do we defend ourselves and our friends against the bullies?"

"You don't."

"But we have a truce," Thomas said. "What if he breaks the truce?"

"The truce is only your word against his," Dad said. "The restraining order is on paper. It's legal and binding."

Another Attack

The first thing Dad had to do that day was take Thomas back to Lake Farm and talk to the head administrator, Mr. Theodore Campbell. Because I was also listed on the restraining order, he let me come along so the man could see that I was no criminal.

Mr. Campbell had phoned my dad before Dad had a chance to call him.

"We put this young man in your care very frequently," he said. "Weekly for more than a year and often for overnight. You're a deputy sheriff, and you allow him to get into trouble serious enough to result in a restraining order?"

"I'd like to come and talk to you about it."

"I should think you would," Mr. Campbell said.

Before we left home, Dad changed into his uniform. "I want him to sense how seriously we take this," he said.

"Aren't you just going to tell him it's crazy?"

"If I did that, he might not let Thomas stay with us anymore. I don't want him to get the idea that any of us are hotheads. He needs to know that Thomas—and you—have been doing the right thing."

I wasn't sure I had been doing the right things, though I knew Thomas had. "Should I say anything?"

"Not unless he asks you something directly," Dad said. "Just tell him the truth. I have to tell you, I'll bet he's trying to decide whether to keep Thomas from coming over again at all."

That started to sink in when we pulled into the long Lake Farm drive. The thought of Thomas not coming over again began to work on my mind. I had already lost a big brother, and Kate and I didn't have much in common. I had the other junior deputies, of course, but we weren't as close as Thomas and I.

This just had to work, whatever Dad was going to do or say. My life would be boring without Thomas every weekend. Anyway, what would he do about Sunday school and church? He was one of the best Christians I knew, certainly more grown-up about it than I was, but I knew he had to keep meeting with other Christians and learning, or even he could fall away.

We were asked to wait for about twenty minutes while Mr. Campbell met with a couple of high school Lake Farmers and their legal guardians.

Thomas whispered what he knew about their stories. They had been caught stealing stuff from the high school store. "Pencils and candy bars mostly," he said.

"What would Mr. Campbell be telling them?" Dad asked.

"That there are no second chances here. They just won't keep lawbreakers around. One more time for each of them, and they'll be gone."

"He may say the same for you," Dad said.

"But I haven't done anything wrong."

"I know. But Thomas, this is what could be described as having had a brush with the law. The legal system is aware of you, has your and Toby's names on file. You don't have a record, but you have to follow a specific order. If you don't . . . well, you know."

"Would I go to jail?"

"I doubt it. The jails, even for juveniles, are full. And this would be your first offense, right?"

"Right."

"For sure you would go to court and maybe to trial. Of course, if you violated a restraining order, the only thing you could do was plead guilty. I mean, there wouldn't be much argument about that. If you pled guilty and threw yourself on the mercy of the court, you might get supervision."

"Which means what?"

"Probation. One false move, and you go to the juvenile detention and correction center."

"I've heard about it," Thomas said. "No way."

"Then you have no thoughts about getting within 200 feet of Ryan?"

"I never did before. He always found us."

"Not when you were defending Kate."

"True, but I was protecting someone. I'd do it again."

"You can't. Don't you see? If you didn't have a ton of witnesses claiming that you had no choice, you'd wind up in the juvenile home."

Thomas shook his head and looked down.

I was getting scared. "Would they lock me up, Dad?"

"Same thing goes for you, Toby. Of course, you've never even been in trouble for fighting before, but a restraining order is serious business."

"It's so unfair," I said. "You know the story. You know we're telling the truth. How Ryan can get one of those put out on us is ridiculous."

"A lot is ridiculous about how the system works nowadays," my dad said. "People can sue each other over anything. So it shouldn't really be surprising that a bully hassles you guys and ambushes you and then puts out a restraining order on you when you surprise him when he's alone."

We were called into Mr. Campbell's office. I was nervous. His office was large, and he seemed very formal. He was a big man with a gravelly voice, but he seemed friendly enough, shaking hands all around.

He offered us chairs and then sat behind his desk. "First, Mr. Andrews," he said, "I want to thank you and both boys here for the help you were with that unfortunate experience we had with Max Carney. At least Max Carney was the name I knew him by all these years. Dreadful business, and I'm glad to be rid of him before he caused us any more embarrassment —or worse."

Thomas and I had helped catch a man who had worked at Lake Farm for years. He was using a phony name and actually had two wives and two families in different cities and had done things like that before.

But Mr. Campbell suddenly grew serious. "I don't enjoy having to come into the office on a weekend. Unfortunately, I had another problem that needed my attention, but I like to run a clean operation here. People expect my kids to be model citizens, and to the best of my ability I'm going to guarantee that.

"I kind of liked Thomas having exposure to a fine family like yours, Mr. Andrews. I understand you take him to church too, and I'm all for that. Not enough of our kids get to rub shoulders with normal families, especially those of law enforcement officers. But you understand that I cannot allow him in a situation that will get him arrested or in some kind of trouble that will be bad for him and for the Home."

"I understand," Dad said.

I wondered why Dad didn't explain everything and let Mr. Campbell know how stupid the restraining order was. He always had his reasons, though. He understood adults way better than I did. He must have known, or guessed, that Mr. Campbell would eventually ask for his side of the story.

"I have to make a decision here," Mr. Campbell said. "As you know, the weekly decision to permit young Mr. Christian here to stay with you is not made at my level. There are supervisors and counselors who make those kinds of determinations. But in the end I answer for everything that happens here. If Thomas violates this restraining order and gets arrested and charged and goes to trial, I'm going to be hard-pressed to answer why I permitted him to go back into the same situation that started it."

"I understand fully," Dad said. "I'll continue to take full responsibility for the boy every minute he's in our care, and there will be no violating of the restraining order."

"Well, thank you for that," Mr. Campbell said, "but I still need to know how this thing all came about in the first place. How do a pair of twelve year olds get to the place where someone asks for such an order on them?"

I wanted Dad to tell the story. It was obvious that Mr. Campbell liked and trusted him. He didn't know me, and it seemed he didn't really know Thomas that well either. Of course, he was probably too busy to get to know every kid in the place.

But Dad looked at the two of us. "I think they should tell it in their own words."

I didn't want to say anything because I would have messed up everything. I was still angry. I would have begun with how stupid I thought it all was, but that would not have given Mr. Campbell a good feeling.

Leave it to Old Tom to tell the whole story, including all the reasons we were trying to be loving to these guys instead of beating them up! I mean, he told it all.

When Thomas was finished, Mr. Campbell looked at me. "Is that the way you remember it?"

I nodded. "Exactly."

"Well, those people are awful," he said. "And a lawyer at that! Of course, that doesn't give you the right to violate the restraining order now. You understand that, right?"

We both agreed.

"And if your father continues to take full responsibility while Thomas is with you, I won't put any restrictions on that."

Thomas and I slapped hands, but my dad shushed us, and Mr. Campbell told us we shouldn't celebrate too early either.

"Do you boys know what 'zero tolerance' means?" he asked.

We shook our heads.

"It means what I said earlier to two other Lake Farm boys. No second chances. This restraining order thing sounds ridiculous, but it's still legal, and you have to abide by it. You can't be simply deciding it's wrong, so you don't have to obey it. Are we clear on that?"

I nodded, but he was looking directly at Thomas, the one he really had responsibility for.

Thomas agreed too.

That wasn't the last meeting we had that day with an adult. When we got back to my house, Daniel Jackson and his father were waiting for us. Daniel's black face was puffy from crying, and his father was angry.

My mother had had just about enough. She pulled Dad and me off to the side before we met with them.

"This has gone too far," she said. "You've let these boys try to handle things themselves, and it hasn't worked. Now I'm tired of worrying about my kids and their friends. If you have to identify these bullies and get them arrested, do it."

"You've got to trust me to handle this, hon," Dad said.

Mom nodded, but she didn't look like she was up for any more surprises.

"I want some arrests made," Mr. Jackson said, his usual

good humor nowhere to be seen. "I'm not gonna have my boy terrorized by bullies and just sit back and take it. And neither is my dog."

"Your dog?" Dad said. "Spike?"

Daniel laughed out loud. "You should have seen him! When those guys ran my bike off the road and I smacked one of them, man, that dog just about jumped the fence. He would have torn them to pieces—you know he would!"

I couldn't believe Daniel was laughing when he had obviously been attacked by the bullies. But I wanted to hear the story. "Was Ryan in on it?" I asked. "Because if he was, after making a truce with us and taking out a restraining order on us—"

"No," Daniel said, and his father scowled every time Daniel smiled, "but it was great. Well, Thomas won't think it was so great, because I didn't tell them I loved them or forgave them or was praying for them. Anyway, here's what happened. They must have been just waiting and watching for me—those other two guys, not Ryan."

"Matt and Andre," Thomas said.

"Right," Daniel said. "So anyway, my mom sends me to the store for milk, right? I ride up there and get it, and I see these guys."

"They weren't hiding?"

"Well, they were supposed to be, I think, but I saw them around the corner of the building. I thought about calling you guys, but I didn't know what they were up to. I didn't even know if they had seen me or were waiting for me or what. They couldn't have known I was going to the store. Maybe they waited closer to my house and then circled around and followed me when I left the store."

"So get to it," I said. "What happened?"

"Like I said, I thought about calling you guys while I was in the store."

"We weren't home anyway."

"But I didn't. I just bought the gallon of milk—I can handle one on my bike. And I'm thinking, *If those guys haven't seen me yet, I don't want 'em to.* Ryan wasn't around, but there were still those two, and they're older and bigger. Well, older. So I decide to just pay for the milk, hop on my bike, and light out of there as fast as I can toward home. I'm a little less than a mile away, you know."

"We know."

"So I head up the hill on Twenty-first Street, cross Green Bay Road, and here they come. Both of 'em, pedaling like mad to catch up. I can't put both hands on the handlebars for good leverage, so they catch me pretty quick. As I get to Waverly, they pull up on each side of me. I acted like I didn't even see them. I'm just looking straight toward my street, and I'm picking up a little speed going down the hill toward Cornell."

"Yeah, then what?"

"Then they start bumping into me—not hard, just enough to get me wobbling—and they start talkin' to me."

"Talking to you?"

"Yeah, they're sayin' stuff like, 'We've got a message from Ryan. His truce doesn't apply to us. You're the last junior deputy to go down,' all that stuff."

"What did you do?"

"Well, I was scared, but I was also mad. I said, 'Yeah? Well, I don't know anything about any truce, and I'm not goin' down.' I start swingin' that gallon of milk at those guys, and they swerve to get out of the way."

I laughed at the thought of it, and that made Daniel cackle.

Even his father had to smile.

"That made me wobble all the more, but when they moved out of my way a little, I was able to get up a little more speed and straighten out. But now I'm going too fast to make the turn at Cornell, and here they come again. I said,

'I'll knock you over, I swear I will.' I'm sorry, Thomas, but givin' them the Christian thing right then just didn't seem the right thing to do. My dad says it's more blessed to give than to receive, and I wanted to make sure I was givin' and not receivin'."

That time even my dad was laughing.

"I didn't want to go on down Waverly, because then they would have me where they wanted me, and I didn't want to drop that milk either. I've done that before, and it doesn't go over so big with my mom. So I slammed on the brakes, and they went past me. I jumped off the bike and started running with the bike in the other direction, my left hand on the handlebars and my right holding the milk with one finger on the handlebar.

"By the time they turned around, I was on Cornell and heading home. Spike could see me from his pen behind the garage, and he was barkin' and carryin' on as usual, scolding me for not taking him with me. I should have, but he's not allowed in the store.

"I get almost to the front of my house when they come up on both sides of me again, and I start swingin' that gallon. I bopped the shorter, heavier one—"

"Andre," Thomas said.

"Yeah, Andre. I got him right in the shoulder and made his bike flip over, and he went rollin' in the ditch. If Spike had known he could jump the fence, he would have eaten that boy alive. But while I was watching Andre, who didn't get hurt that bad, the other one, the tall one—"

"Matt."

"Yea, Matt. He rammed right into me and knocked my bike over. I dropped the milk and landed on it, and it broke open."

"Ouch!"

"It didn't hurt that bad! Just a bruised rib. But the funny thing was that with a hole in the plastic carton and me landing on it, it shot most of that gallon of milk all over Matt. Man, was he mad! His bike went wobbling into the ditch on the other side of the road, and when he tried to get up, I ran over and slugged him right in the neck."

"Good shot."

"I was aimin' for his face. Spike was goin' crazy! He wanted those guys so bad. But I was outnumbered, and they both rammed at me with their bikes as they rode off, Andre rubbing his shoulder, Matt rubbing his neck and dripping milk. I had to answer to my mother for that milk—but, man, it was worth it. I only wish Spike had been out."

I had to admit I wished the same thing. I knew Thomas wanted to try the peaceful approach, but so far that wasn't working.

Now What?

Dad told Mr. Jackson all about the restraining order, which didn't seem to make Daniel's dad any calmer.

"I want to do the right thing here," he said, "but I need to know if this was a racial thing. Don't these kids know how bad it can look for them in this day and age when two white boys attack a black kid?"

"Oh, I'm sure it's not racial," Dad said. "They terrorized Joel McBride first, then Thomas Christian, then Jonathan Bynum, then Kate, before they got to Daniel."

"You know what that means, don't you?" Mr. Jackson said. "Your boy has to be next."

"They as much as said so when they were threatening Thomas and Toby the other day. It was like they were saving the junior deputy captain until last. I don't know what they're going to do about the restraining order, though. If Thomas and Toby can't come within two hundred feet of this Ryan kid, he can't get near them either."

"Well," Daniel said, "maybe they'll just send Matt and Andre again. Toby could take them. I almost did."

"You're a lot bigger than I am," I said. "And you were carrying a weapon."

"A weapon?"

"A gallon of milk!"

And everyone laughed.

"But seriously, I wouldn't want to take those guys on. I've got to keep track of Kate on the way to and from school every day, and I can't expect you guys to be around all the time. Thomas is usually at our house only on weekends."

Mr. Jackson sighed. "It's too bad this big kid, the leader—"

"Ryan."

"Right. It's too bad he didn't take you and Thomas up on your offer of friendship. We all know that was the right approach. Those guys could have saved face and maybe learned something."

"We should keep trying to get to know them," Thomas said.

"I don't know," Dad said. "They have a problem with you guys, and they don't want to talk it through. From what you told me about your little meeting with Ryan, he didn't trust you. He thought you were going to pay him back for what he did to you, so he offered that truce to save his own skin. Then he turned around and had his father slap a temporary restraining order on you."

"Then what should we do?" Thomas asked.

"Protect yourselves," Dad said. "Be smart. But don't attack. Remember, they are the ones with the problem, not you. You don't have a problem with them."

"We do now, Dad," I said. "Now that they've ambushed almost every one of us."

"But Thomas is right, Toby," Dad said. "It's not our place to get revenge. That's God's job. If you fight them back, other than to just defend yourself or somebody else, you're putting yourself on the same level as they are, and that's pretty low."

"I know we all want to do the right thing," I said, "but don't forget I'm the only victim left. I'm going to be next. I can't take Matt and Andre by myself, and who knows whether Ryan will be there or not? I know he's not supposed to be, but if they get me alone and Matt and Andre swear he wasn't there, who would know different?"

Mr. Jackson stood and looked out the window. When he turned back, he spoke more softly than I had ever heard him. "Let me tell you something," he said. "I know what the right thing is to do. But right now I'm still so mad that my boy was attacked for no reason that I know I wouldn't do the right thing if I saw those two kids. I expect I'll get over this in time. But I'm going to teach Daniel how to defend himself. I won't be letting him attack them back, but if they ever try anything on him again, they'll regret it. They'll go home with more than a scrape or clothes full of milk. Is that unreasonable?"

"No," my dad said. "I admire Thomas trying to make his faith part of how he treats people, especially people who treat him badly. I think he's tried in several ways to convince these bullies that he doesn't hate them, that he's praying for them, and that he doesn't want to be their enemy. But I agree with you in that I don't think God would expect the boys to just stand there and get beat up."

Thomas's face looked cold and stony. He had been sitting thinking for a long time, ever since he heard what happened to Daniel. It was great that Daniel still had a sense of humor about it, but still I knew he would be afraid to be out alone, and his run-in with Matt and Andre would bother him for a long time.

Finally, Thomas spoke. "This really bothers me. I don't understand why this doesn't work. A soft answer is supposed to turn away wrath. Love is supposed to conquer everything. I felt better being beat up and still telling those guys they weren't my enemies than I did knocking Ryan over when he was trying to run down Kate. Why can't we get through to these guys?"

"I'm going to tell you what I think," Dad said, "but of course it's just my opinion. You have to keep in mind that I'm a police officer and that I see the bad side of life every day. But I'm also a Christian, as are my family members and the Jacksons and you, Thomas. And after I tell my idea, I'm going to also tell you what I think you should do next. But you're getting old enough to make these decisions yourself and to live with the consequences. The only thing I will forbid you to do, because you're under my authority when you're away from Lake Farm, and because I promised Mr. Campbell, is to violate that restraining order.

"I don't think you should counterattack. I don't think we should have these kids arrested. I—"

"I do," Mr. Jackson said.

"I know you do, friend, and it's hard to argue with you when your son was roughed up. I just think we still need to let the kids handle this. Let them grow up and take care of their own problems. I wouldn't put up with much more from these bullies, and we have to come up with something that teaches them a lesson if they try anything more."

"I don't mean any disrespect," Mr. Jackson said, "but you might feel different if your son had been attacked."

"Maybe. But in a way he already has been. My daughter was scared and probably would have been hurt if Thomas and Toby hadn't rescued her. And Toby was hurt in that scuffle. So far, what we have are bullies getting away with bullying. The best cure for that is for someone to stand up to them."

"See?" Thomas said. "That's what I mean. I thought we weren't supposed to pay back evil for evil."

"We aren't. If you guys ambushed them—and hardly anyone would say you don't have the right to do that—you would be repaying evil with evil, and like I said, you'd be putting yourselves on their level. The best thing you've done so far is to show them you're not afraid, that you won't be pushed around."

"But I still want to know," Thomas said, "why they haven't changed when we've been nice to them."

"That's what I'm going to try to explain," my dad said. "I think what you boys are getting here, admittedly in a painful way, is a picture of how God treats us and how we treat Him."

"Huh?"

"See, from God's point of view, *we* are the bullies. *We* are the enemy. He loves us and wants to befriend us, to do loving things for us, to save us, to make us His children. And what do we do? Most of us thumb our noses at Him. We keep doing what we want to do. We ignore Him, or sometimes we even shake our fists in His face. People who sin when they know better are mocking God.

"I believe God gently tries to draw unbelievers to Himself. I think He's harder on Christians. Those who believe in Him and call themselves His children can't just live as they please. He wants them back with Him, and I think God disciplines them to bring them back."

"So He's easier on the sinners?" Thomas said. "Is that what you mean?"

"I'm no theologian," Dad said, "but I think that's right. He invites unbelievers to Himself—and once they're there, He sometimes has to let difficult things happen to them if they stray away."

Thomas shrugged and nodded. "I guess that makes sense. But what does that have to do with the East Side bullies?"

"Don't you see how frustrating it is for God by what you're going through? Of course, you're not God, but you have the best intentions about these boys, right?"

We all nodded.

"You don't want to be their enemies. You want to be their friends. You may not like them or the people that they are, but you haven't done anything to make them hate you. Still, they do. When you respond to their violence and anger with love and forgiveness, they get worse.

"That's what God has to deal with all the time. Yes, a soft answer *will* turn away wrath more often than a cross answer will. And love will draw more people than harshness will. But we have a free will. We will respond to God in whatever way we choose. And the East Side bullies have responded to you in the way they choose. Frankly, I wouldn't want to be in their shoes right now."

"Why?"

"Because they have chosen a dangerous path. They have chosen to ignore your attempts to make friends. Now they have to live with that. They have a lawyer friend who can put out a restraining order on you, but you have a deputy sheriff who can keep an eye on them and arrest them if they break the law.

"People who ignore God have to fend for themselves. And bullies who ignore acts of friendship are in for trouble."

"So what do we do, and what's going to happen?"

Dad laughed. "I can't predict the future," he said. "But my advice is to be smart, be careful, stick together, defend each other, don't attack, and watch these guys destroy themselves. You do the right thing because it's the right thing. Might doesn't make right. Right is right, and good always wins over evil. I know it sounds a little holy, but I say do what you know is right and watch God work it out."

Living in Fear

The Kalamazoo County Junior Deputies met in the old coal bin in our basement the next afternoon after church and Sunday dinner. Big Dan brought his German shepherd, Spike, who was—of course—the center of attention.

Daniel was still in a pretty good mood, considering what had happened to him the day before. His ribs were still sore, but he bragged about what he would do to Matt and Andre if he ever saw them again.

"What your dog would do, you mean," Jonathan said.

"Spike sure wanted to get in on that action," Daniel said.

"What would he do?" I asked.

"He'd tear 'em to shreds," he said, and he was serious. "This dog was trained in Germany."

"Why doesn't he hurt us?" I asked.

"Because he can tell we're friends. If he thought you were trying to hurt me, he'd turn on you in a minute. Try it."

"What do you mean, try it?"

"Like push me or yell at me or something."

"I don't want to get attacked."

"Don't worry," Daniel said. "I'll call him off. Sometimes when Spike is in the house and we have a visitor, he'll bark and growl and look threatening until my dad shakes the person's hand."

Everyone fell silent, especially Kate, who was a little shy around the huge dog anyway. When everyone else petted him, she held back. Sometimes he eyed her carefully too, I thought.

The dog perked up his ears because all the attention seemed turned on Daniel and me, with everyone waiting to see what we would do.

Daniel said, "I'll just shout at you, and you shout back and push my shoulder. Then I'll make sure Spike knows I'm OK."

"Are you sure?" I said.

"Yes! He's trained!"

"OK," I said.

"Hey!" Daniel shouted suddenly.

"Hey, yourself!" I shouted and bumped him in the shoulder.

Spike leaped into attack position and growled, then barked loud at me, which made Kate scream.

When she screamed, the dog turned on her and barked louder, as if he was ready to snap at her. She jumped from her chair and tried to get away, and Spike jumped toward her.

I hollered, "Daniel, do something!"

All the other guys were moving around too. In the confusion the dog was going crazy, ready to attack someone but not sure who.

"Spike!" Daniel shouted. "Sit!"

The dog sat but still stared at Kate and barked.

Everyone was keeping his distance.

"Good dog," Daniel said, stroking the dog's head. "Look, Spike, he's a friend."

Daniel and I shook hands, but still Spike stared at Kate, who was crying.

"Come here, Kate," Daniel said.

"No!"

"Just come over here quietly and shake hands with me. Then Spike will let you pet him."

"I don't want to."

"I really think you should," Daniel said. "He's suspicious of you because you screamed."

"You come over here and shake hands," Kate said. "I'm not getting near that dog."

"Spike, stay," Daniel said, holding up a finger in front of Spike's face. And Daniel moved over to shake Kate's hand. "Spike, come," he said, and when Kate tensed he said, "Just relax and be calm around him."

The dog rose and walked slowly to Daniel, who still held Kate's hand in his brown fingers.

"Spike, shake," he said, and Spike held up one paw, looking into Kate's eyes.

She smiled and shook the dog's paw, then petted his neck, and he nuzzled her.

Pretty soon everyone was shaking Spike's paw, and that dog's tail was wagging like everything.

"He'll defend any of us now," Daniel said, "but we should not confuse him by everybody giving him commands. And don't anybody try to feed him. He's trained to attack anybody who offers him food except our family."

"Why?"

"Because a lot of burglars and criminals have learned they can keep a guard dog quiet by tossing him chunks of meat. These dogs are trained to kill if the wrong person feeds them."

We had so much fun with the dog that we hardly got any business done. Mostly we just talked about the fact that I would likely be the next victim if the East Side bullies tried anything new. We had no idea whether Ryan would get near Thomas or me after having the restraining order put out on us. Joel was worried that we couldn't protect everybody.

"You're keeping track of Kate. Thomas still walks home with the other Lake Farmers, but they weren't much help last time. Jonathan and Daniel and I can pretty much hang with each other. But who's gonna protect you, Toby?"

"I will," Kate said. "I'm not lettin' anybody hurt my brother."

"What're you gonna do, Kate," Jonathan said, "scare 'em off by screaming?"

"It might work," Kate said, and we had to agree. Her screaming had sure spooked the dog.

"I'll have time to walk home with Toby and Kate before I go to the Home," Thomas said.

"Yeah, you'd have time," I said. "But then you're not with the rest of your guys, and you wind up walking alone."

"I don't mind."

"I do," I said. "I think we all do."

Everyone nodded.

"Listen," Jonathan said, "nothing's gonna happen tomorrow anyway, because we get out before lunch. It's some kind of special day for the teachers. We ought to meet over here again."

I didn't want to look too eager about that, because I didn't want to admit to the others that I was scared to death. I knew I was next, and I didn't want to get ganged up on, beat up, run off the road, or anything like that. Frankly, I was worried about Kate and me with no one to help. I wanted Thomas to walk with us, but I didn't want him to go home alone after that.

The idea of another junior deputy meeting the next afternoon after our school was out sounded great to me. I let the others get excited about it so it would be their idea and not mine. Then I checked with my mother to see if it would be all right.

"Their school gets out early?" she said. "I think Estes Junior High is in their district. Let me check with your aunt and see if your cousin gets out early tomorrow too."

It was true. Estes would be letting out early too. I realized then that if anything was going to happen, it would probably happen the next day.

I wanted to be brave. Some people thought of all of us as heroes because of some of the cases we had solved. I wanted to live up to the name of junior deputy, but I couldn't shake the feeling of dread.

When I told the guys about Estes, they all agreed that at least Matt and Andre would probably try to ambush Kate and me, since they would have plenty of time to get over to our neighborhood.

"Yeah, but we'll have plenty of time too," Jonathan said. "I think we should plan on hiding out along your route home, and we'll be watching just in case. No matter where they attack, we'll be there."

"I wouldn't mind getting back at those guys," Little Joel said.

"I don't want you fightin' 'em," Thomas said. "Your job should be to get Kate home fast if anything happens. It would be too easy for her to get hurt."

"What will the rest of us do?" Daniel said.

"Well," Thomas began—it looked like a plan was already forming in his mind—"I'll pretend to start home with the other Lake Farmers, but I'll double back around and be in position somewhere along the way too. Probably the best place for us will be up in that big tree two blocks from your house. They'll never think of that, and they'll probably be on their bikes again."

"Great idea!" Jonathan said. "I love to climb trees, and we can bomb them with stuff if we need to."

"Like what?"

"Like stuff that wouldn't kill them but would knock them

over or knock their bikes down. If they ever left their bikes, we should hide them good and make those guys walk to get home."

Daniel told how he and some friends had once made a swing by hanging an old tire from a high limb. "We got tired of that after a while," he said, "so we started putting things in front of the tire and then swinging it until it hit them. We'd knock over bikes, people, toys, whatever."

"Cool! Can you bring that?"

"Sure! We'd have to be careful to just swing it and not drop it, because it could kill somebody."

"What else can we do?"

"I'll bring water balloons," Jonathan said.

"There are all kinds of ideas," Thomas said. "Why don't you let us surprise you? When you think you're really in for it, we'll come swooping down out of the big tree to rescue you. Joel will run Kate home, and we'll make sure the bullies don't bother any of us again."

"No more loving them and praying for them and all that, Thomas?"

"Sure, but we're just waiting and watching to be sure they don't hurt anyone."

The Junior Deputies spent the rest of the afternoon planning their defense. By the time our meeting was over, I think everybody was hoping the bullies *would* attack us. Everybody but me. I trusted my friends, and I was pretty sure I'd be the best-protected deputy of all of them. But I didn't want to face the Leathers if I didn't have to.

It was fun to watch Joel going over his part. He knew that at his age and size he was no match for the junior high bullies. But he also knew he could outrun anybody, and Kate was fast too. Besides, we all knew he thought Kate was pretty cute, and the idea of rescuing her and making sure she got home safely made him smile.

That night while we were on our way to take Thomas

back to Lake Farm, we told my parents all our plans. Mom agreed that Joel and Jonathan and Daniel could come to our house after their school let out and work out of our headquarters in the coal bin.

Thomas and I talked about how Kate and I should take our normal route home. “Make it easy for them,” he said. “That’ll make our job easier too.”

“I’m going to be glad when this is over,” I said. “I don’t think I can stand it anymore.”

“Well, like your dad said, we have to show them we can stand up to them. Bullies can only bully people who are afraid of them.”

That didn’t make me feel much better, because I was the only one who knew I was afraid of the East Side bullies. I didn’t want to be, but I was ready to do whatever I had to do to make them back off.

The next day was torture. I couldn’t keep my mind on my classes, and my attention span was zero. Kate and I were going to meet at the main entrance and hurry home. We’d keep our eyes open but try to look normal.

About twenty minutes before school let out I was called to the principal’s office over the loudspeaker.

What now? I rushed down there to find that my mother was on the phone.

“Toby,” she said, “the other deputies are all in place, so you should be safe. Make sure Kate gets home if anything happens. I’ll find a reason to be in the backyard and watching for her. And, Toby, your friends wanted me to tell you that something is definitely going to happen.”

“They did? Did they see the bullies?”

“No, but they found their bikes.”

“Really? Where?”

“Stashed in the bushes along the way.”

"What do the guys make of that? Where are the East Siders?"

"They think they'll probably be on foot, somewhere near the school, so don't get away from the crowd or go anywhere new. They must be thinking that if they can get you to run, they'll just jump on their bikes and track you down. But they won't be able to."

"Why not?"

"Because your friends got to those bikes."

"They hid them?"

"Better than that. They made them temporarily useless."

"What's that mean?"

"You'll see."

The Last Showdown

When the final bell rang, I raced to my locker, having set the lock so I would have to turn it only to the last number and it would pop open. I stashed my stuff, got my jacket, and hurried to where Kate was already waiting. I could tell I was more worried than she was. If I didn't know better, I would have thought she had forgotten all about the danger ahead of us. I didn't tell her about Mom's phone call.

As we left the building, Kate wanted to stop and talk to a friend.

I couldn't believe it. I said, "No, Kate, now come on. You know we have to get straight home today."

As we crossed Oakland Drive, I caught sight of Thomas walking toward Lake Farm with lots of the other kids from there.

At the last instant, just before we turned off Oakland, I glanced back at the big group of Lake Farmers and saw Thomas peeking back at me. He nodded slightly, telling me the plan was on and that he would soon be breaking free and circling around until he wasn't far behind us.

It was then that Matt and Andre stepped out from behind some big bushes. Matt walked next to me, and Andre next to Kate, and suddenly I realized that this was it. They had made their move. In their minds, I was going down today.

"What do you guys want?" I said, continuing to walk. Kate took my hand.

"What do you think we want, captain?" Matt said. "It's your turn, deputy."

"Then you don't need Kate here."

"Kate can stay right where she is," Andre said.

So I talked directly to him. "If you want to walk with us, you're welcome, but you're not going to walk next to Kate."

He laughed, so I stopped. "I'm serious," I said, and I was getting mad. "You can try anything you want with me, but you leave her alone, and you don't walk next to her."

He could see I meant it, and he looked at Matt, who motioned him away from Kate with a nod. "What do you mean, try anything we want with you?"

"I should be asking you that," I said. "What do you want from me?"

I kept walking quickly, wanting to get closer to the block where I knew my friends would be watching from the big tree.

"You know what we want," Matt said. "But there's someone who'd like to talk to you."

That made me curious. Somebody new? Or Ryan? I didn't want Kate around to find out. We were within a block and a half of where Joel would join Kate and run her on home.

I said to Kate, "Now!" and we both took off running.

Matt and Andre probably could have caught us if *they'd* tried running, but they already had their bike plan, and I knew all about it. Kate and I were sprinting full speed down

Amherst Avenue heading toward Barnard when—I learned later—Matt went to one side of the street and Andre went to another.

They pulled their bikes from their hiding places and jumped aboard, but when they tried pedaling they just fanned the air. Their chains had been disconnected from the sprockets, and until they could turn the bikes over and repair them, they were getting nowhere.

I saw Joel was waiting about a half block up, and I told Kate to head straight for him. Joel grabbed her hand and took off with her toward our house. *I* headed straight for the big tree.

When I was under it, I turned to get a look at Matt and Andre and to guess how long it would take their strong, long strides to catch up. Then I turned back around and saw Ryan closing in from the other direction.

"Oh, now look what you've done," he said. "You've violated a court order. You weren't supposed to come within two hundred feet of me. Now you're in real trouble."

"I have the right to walk home the same way I do every day," I said. "I didn't come within two hundred feet of you. You're the one out of your neighborhood."

Matt and Andre came sliding to a stop on their sneakers in the gravel.

"So now finally it's just the three of us and you," Ryan said. "Any last words?"

"Last words?" I said, no longer afraid. I realized I had dreaded not knowing how it was all going to happen. Now that I was in the middle of it, and the bike part had already gone our way, I knew I had help somewhere, and this wasn't going to go the way Ryan thought it was. "What do you think you're going to do, kill me?"

"You might wish we had when we're finished with you," Ryan said.

"Then, yeah, I've got some words," I said. "I want you

guys to know that we don't hate you. We pray for you. We think we could even get to like each other. I should warn you to give this up, because God will protect me."

"I've heard enough," Ryan said. "Let's take him."

"I don't think so," Thomas said, seeming to come out of nowhere. All three of the bullies looked shocked to see him. Now it was only three against two.

"I don't think so either!" I heard from above, and everyone looked up. There, hanging onto an old tire and a long length of rope was not Daniel, whose tire swing it was, but Jonathan. He shouted, "Geronimo!" and came swinging down in a huge arc.

If it hadn't been such a dangerous situation, I would have laughed. He was wearing a football helmet, with his red hair sticking out the ear holes and the bottom. And he had a newspaper carrier's bag filled with water balloons.

I think his plan was to bang into the Leathers as he swung through, but he either hadn't practiced or didn't have any way to steer, and he simply sailed by. The bullies were so surprised they just watched him swing back and forth, stepping out of his way each time.

Jonathan looked embarrassed and started throwing water balloons, but as many of them hit Thomas and me as hit the East Siders.

Still, it was a great surprise attack. As Jonathan swung up toward the tree again, he pushed off the trunk with his feet and came shooting back down toward us again. This time he smacked into Andre, making him fall and roll over into the gravel.

Matt charged Jonathan, knocking him out of the tire, and the bag and the rest of the water balloons went flying and breaking and splashing all over the place.

At least now it was three against three. I wondered where Daniel was. He obviously had provided the tire swing, but I didn't see him anywhere.

While Jonathan was on the ground, Matt ripped off his helmet and got him in a headlock.

Jonathan squealed, but as I moved to help him, Ryan grabbed me and threw me to the ground. I couldn't believe how big and strong he was. He slid around and gripped me from behind and put a choke hold on me too. I was afraid I would pass out from lack of air, and I could see Andre charging Thomas.

Thomas was pretty tough and holding his own, but Andre was the heaviest and strongest of the junior highers, and he seemed to be winning.

I was mad and frantic, and I'd had more than enough. I thrashed around and rolled to get my neck free so I could gulp in some air. And it was then that I saw Daniel, beautiful Daniel. He came running down the street from my house, and what should he have at the end of a leash but Spike, the huge German shepherd.

Spike was straining and pulling Daniel so fast toward the action that it was all Dan could do to keep his balance. He was shouting something about "Our friends, Spike! Get 'em!"

And Spike was ready to do just that. The dog broke free and charged the three fighters, starting with Jonathan and Matt.

As soon as Matt heard the barking and snarling, he let Jonathan up and ran as fast as he could the other way.

Thomas had flipped Andre over and was trying to hold his arms to keep him from punching when Spike began circling them, barking madly.

Andre rolled into the ditch to get away from the dog, and soon he was headed toward Matt, and they were grabbing their chainless bikes and running back to the East Side.

Ryan seemed not to pay attention to the dog. He had the drop on me. He kept going back to a choke hold every time I wriggled free.

But by now Spike was a spinning and charging mass of

muscle and fur, eager to devour somebody. Matt and Andre were gone, and Thomas and Jonathan were safe. Only Ryan and I were still fighting, and I could see that Ryan was Spike's next target.

I fought to get to my feet, and Ryan made the mistake of grabbing my jacket at the shoulders and twirling me around and throwing me up against a tree.

With that Spike came driving at Ryan in full fury.

The mighty dog nipped at his heels and his seat, and I saw the bully's eyes grow wide with terror. It was as if he knew he was dog food if he didn't do something right now. Ryan tried climbing me to get away from the dog.

I had never seen such a look of fright on a person's face, and suddenly, in spite of all he had done to us, I felt sorry for him. I cupped my hands and put them down by my knees. He stepped into them and straightened his leg, catapulting himself up into the fork of the tree, from which he climbed out onto a safe branch.

But nothing was stopping the enraged Spike. He had lost three targets, but there I was, alone and defenseless in front of him. His paws hit my face, and I felt flesh tearing away from my eyebrow and blood running down my face. Then Spike sank his teeth into my arm, right through the jacket and shirt and flesh.

As he yanked me to the ground, I shouted, along with Daniel and Thomas, "Spike! No! Friend!"

And as if Spike realized what he had done, he immediately went from scratching and biting to trying to lick me. I didn't want that, and Daniel quickly grabbed his leash, pulled him away, and calmed him down.

"Get that dog out of here!" Ryan said from his perch in the tree. He was crying. When Daniel hauled his dog toward our house, Ryan jumped out of the tree and ran away.

The next afternoon, as I lay in Borgess Hospital after

minor surgery and lots of stitches in my forehead and arm, a nurse told me I had a visitor. I sure hoped it was Thomas. But it wasn't. He would come later.

Ryan came quietly and shyly through the door and sat down, not saying anything at first.

I said hi.

"I don't know what to say," he said. "I don't know why you did it, and maybe I'll never understand, but I want to thank you for saving my life. That dog would have killed me."

"I know. I hope you're not gonna have your dad sue Daniel or his family."

Ryan shook his head. "Nah. 'Course not. And we're taking off that restraining order too. If you hadn't been within two hundred feet of me yesterday, *I'd* be the one in the hospital, or in a casket."

I don't know what made me say it, but I said, "I sure wish you'd apologize for all the stuff you did to us."

Ryan shook his head. "I'm not very good at apologies. But I can tell you that we're not gonna hassle you anymore. You've seen the last of us."

"Well, thanks for that," I said. "This hasn't been any fun, at least for us."

"It was for us," Ryan said, "until yesterday. I think we all need a break now. Anyway, thanks for helping me get away from the dog and giving me a boost up that tree. I dreamed about it last night, and I can't quit thinking about it all day."

"Really?" I said.

"Yeah."

"Well, then now maybe you know what it feels like to be bullied. It's not that fun, is it?"

"I guess not."

And Ryan looked like a different kid. He was still older and bigger, but he didn't have that smirk, that sneer, that looking-down-on-people face. Maybe he would go back to being a bully someday. All I knew was that something had given him a view of what it's like to be the victim.

That something, of course, was Daniel's dog, Spike. But it was also Thomas and his interest in doing the right thing because it's the right thing. None of us knew if we would ever again see the East Side bullies, but if we did, we hoped they'd be changed. We hoped they'd be as different inside as Ryan looked on the outside that afternoon.

Moody Press, a ministry of the Moody Bible Institute, is designed for education, evangelization, and edification. If we may assist you in knowing more about Christ and the Christian life, please write us without obligation: Moody Press, c/o MLM, Chicago, Illinois 60610.